The
World
Without
Us

The World Without Us

Robin Stevenson

ORCA BOOK PUBLISHERS

Library and Archives Canada Cataloguing in Publication

Stevenson, Robin, 1968–, author
The world without us / Robin Stevenson.

Issued in print and electronic formats.
ISBN 978-1-4598-0680-1 (pbk.).—ISBN 978-1-4598-0681-8 (pdf).—
ISBN 978-1-4598-0682-5 (epub)

I. Title.
PS8637.T487W67 2015   jc813'.6   C2014-906598-1

First published in the United States, 2015
Library of Congress Control Number: 2014951602

Summary: Mel is tormented by thoughts that she may be responsible for her best friend's suicide attempt.

Orca Book Publishers is dedicated to preserving the environment and has printed this book on Forest Stewardship Council® certified paper.

Orca Book Publishers gratefully acknowledges the support for its publishing programs provided by the following agencies: the Government of Canada through the Canada Book Fund and the Canada Council for the Arts, and the Province of British Columbia through the BC Arts Council and the Book Publishing Tax Credit.

Cover design by Chantal Gabriell
Cover images by iStockphoto.com and Dreamstime.com
Author photo by David Lowes

ORCA BOOK PUBLISHERS
PO Box 5626, STN. B
VICTORIA, BC CANADA
V8R 6S4

ORCA BOOK PUBLISHERS
PO Box 468
CUSTER, WA USA
98240-0468

www.orcabook.com
Printed and bound in Canada.

18 17 16 15 • 4 3 2 1

For Pat Schmatz

Falling

Jeremy stands close to the low concrete barrier that runs for miles along the edge of the Sunshine Skyway Bridge. The wind is whipping his hair back, blowing cool night air and the smell of salt into our faces. He braces his hands against the top of the wall and leans out over the water. "Come over here, Mel!"

The wall only reaches my waist, and when I stand close to it and look down, I feel dizzy, as if sheer gravity could pull me over. Far below, the water is an inky black. I step back, shivering, and look up at Jeremy instead. He is facing into the wind, and I fix his profile in my mind, as if I'm taking a picture: black hair flying away from his high forehead, long slightly beaky nose, parted lips, serious expression. Resolute.

"Jeremy?" I say. My voice sounds strange in my own ears. "We're not really going to do this, are we?"

"Yes." He looks at me. "You know we are."

"I don't know. I never thought we'd take it this far."

"We won't feel a thing. It'll be fast, Mel. Real fast."

I imagine those long seconds of falling, time slowing down, the dark water rushing toward me. Will my life really flash before my eyes? Or is that just a myth?

"Here," Jeremy says. "Take my hand. We'll jump together." He reaches for me. I take his hand in mine and am surprised by how warm it is. With my other hand, I tighten my grip on the metal post of the No Stopping sign we've parked beside.

I guess this is crazy, but I am terrified of falling.

"It'll be okay, Mel," Jeremy says. His voice is so soft, I can barely hear him over the wind blowing through the bridge cables.

"Jeremy." I start to cry. "Stop. Please."

"Have you changed your mind? Because if you have—"

"Maybe," I say. "I don't know." I'm sobbing now. "I don't *know*." Jeremy thinks we'll come back, that we'll be reincarnated. I don't know what I believe. I haven't had dreams like the ones he's had. Mostly, I think that this is all there is: you get one shot, one life, and the only choice is whether you want to live it or not. If we jump, the world will just go on without us.

"Come on," he says. "Let's just do it. Ready?" He lifts one leg, swings it over the wall—

"No. Jeremy…" I grab his arm, and the falling weight of him jerks at me, pulls me forward. Something inside me is screaming *no no no,* and my heart kicks inside my chest so hard it hurts, and it's too late, my feet are lifting off the ground, I'm going to fall…

And then Jeremy's sleeve slips from my hand and I am clinging on, one arm wrapped around the metal pole, my feet kicking and scrabbling for traction on the bridge. I am still here, standing on the edge.

And Jeremy is gone.

I stand there, staring down into the darkness that swallowed him up. I feel like time has stopped. I can't see anything, can't even make out the surface of the water under the bridge. There's just blackness down there, thick and solid.

I could still do it, could still jump…but I already know I won't. I turn away from the barrier and watch car after car flash past. People going about their lives like nothing happened. No one stops. My legs feel like liquid. My breath comes in painful, ragged gasps. Distant sirens get louder, and lights flash red and blue from way down the long line of the bridge. I wait there, frozen, until a police car pulls up and I hear someone shout. I slip down into a crouch, my back to the concrete wall. I am shaking, my whole body trembling, my teeth chattering. Two men in uniform are getting out of the car and one is walking slowly toward me, his hands raised, palms out, as if he is approaching a wild horse and doesn't want to spook it. "It's all right," he says.

But nothing is all right. Nothing will ever be all right. "He jumped," I say. "Jeremy jumped."

"Why don't you get in the car?" he says. He's an older man, with stubbly gray hair and tired eyes. "Out of the wind."

"What about Jeremy?" I say.

"A boat's already gone out to look for him," he says. "Someone saw him jump and called it in."

To look for his body, I think. That's all that's down there. Whatever made him Jeremy is gone. I move toward the car and I can see the cop relax, his arms dropping back to his sides. "He just jumped," I say again. "I didn't think he'd really do it."

"Fourteenth one this year," the second man says. He's leaning against the car, and behind him, the lit-up yellow cables of the bridge slant upward into the night sky, glowing and weirdly beautiful. As I approach, he straightens and opens the back door for me. "Hop in. You'll be warmer."

I slide into the backseat and wrap my arms around myself. The older man gets in beside me, and the younger guy gets in the driver's seat. The doors click locked, and I wonder if they think I am going to dash out and leap over the wall.

Every muscle in my body is vibrating like a tightly strung wire. "I didn't think he meant it," I say again. "I didn't think he'd really do it."

"I'm Officer Jeffers," the cop beside me says. "What's your name?"

"Melody."

"Was it your boyfriend who jumped, Melody?"

I shake my head. "My friend." I am numb. None of this feels real. "His name is Jeremy Weathers."

The cop in the front seat is talking into his radio. He turns to face me. "Do you know his address?"

I picture Jeremy's house: the low, ranch-style bungalow, the palm-tree-dotted expanse of green lawn. "Um, Lakewood Estates," I say. "He lives with his mom... I don't remember the house number, but it's on Desoto near Columbus Way."

The cop relays the information to whomever he is talking to, and I imagine someone driving over there, through the wide dark streets of his subdivision, up his long driveway. A cop knocking on the door, Jeremy's mother answering, dressed in her housecoat, maybe, since they'll be waking her up. She'll see the cop standing there, and she'll feel a sudden clutch of fear.

I wasn't supposed to be here for this part. Jeremy and I never talked about anything after the leap from the bridge. I never thought about what would happen after.

There wasn't supposed to *be* an after.

"The fellow who called it in said you were right there by the wall with the kid who jumped," the older officer—Jeffers—says. "He said it looked like you tried to stop him."

I stare at him blankly, and the two men exchange glances.

"We're going to take you to the hospital." He reaches across me and buckles my seat belt. "Can we call someone to meet us there? Your mom, maybe?"

I close my eyes, and for a moment I wish I had jumped too. Only not really. Because in that moment when Jeremy's weight almost pulled me over with him, in that moment when I thought I was falling, I realized one thing: I didn't want to die. "I want to go home," I say.

"You know, I don't get it," the younger cop says from the front seat. "Couple kids like you two, young, healthy, you got everything to live for. What could be so bad that it'd make you want to die?"

All I can think about is Jeremy, falling.

"What a waste," he says. He starts the engine. "What a goddamn waste."

I'm not sure about this, but I think Jeremy looked up as he fell. I couldn't see his expression—just a glimpse of the pale oval of his face, his open mouth, and then he was gone. Was he saying something? Did he have time to realize that I hadn't jumped, that I had pulled my hand free?

Maybe he didn't look up at all. Maybe I made that memory up. I was panicking, struggling to keep my balance and my grip on the metal pole.

I don't know how reliable memory really is.

≈

I ask the cops to drive me home, but they take me to the hospital instead. Apparently they think I'm a suicide risk, even though I obviously chose not to jump when I had the chance. A nurse ushers me into a tiny room, and one of the cops stands by the door—in case I try to leave, I guess.

"There's a social worker coming down to talk with you," the nurse says. She's an older woman with short gray hair and a name-tag chain threaded with jewel-like beads. "She'll be here in a minute."

"Has anyone called my parents?" I ask.

"No. Would you like me to call them?"

I shake my head quickly. "No. Please don't. But it's past eleven, and they'll be expecting me home soon. Can't I just go home? Please?" My mom's car is still illegally parked on the bridge, I realize. Or maybe it's been towed away by now.

"Let's take things one step at a time," the nurse says.

I lower myself onto a gray plastic chair. The nurse leaves, and I eye the open door. The cop—the younger guy—is still standing there. "Is Jeremy…Do you know if…"

He shakes his head. "Haven't heard anything."

"Hello, Melody?" A woman slips through the open door, ignoring the cop. "I'm Christine. I'm a social worker here. I'd like to talk with you. Is that okay?"

I don't imagine I really have a choice. She pulls up a second chair, sitting a couple of feet away from me. She's youngish, in her twenties, I guess, with shoulder-length brown hair, freckles, huge dark eyes. Her earrings are tiny candy canes. "I imagine you're feeling pretty shaken up right now," she says.

I nod. "Have you heard anything? Did they find…"

"Jeremy? Yes, they did. Melody, he's pretty badly injured." Her voice is soft, cautious.

"He's *alive*?" This hadn't even occurred to me. I hadn't known it was possible to survive that fall.

"Yes. He was brought here—got here just before you did, actually. He didn't lose consciousness when he hit the water, and luckily there was a boater out there who was able to get to him quickly. But he's in serious condition. He's in surgery." She holds my gaze, and her eyes are unreadable. "The police officer said that the two of you were standing on the bridge together. Is that right?"

"I was just...I wanted to talk him out of it. Persuade him not to do it," I say. *God.* What if he'd been hoping I would? Maybe he'd have taken the out if I'd given him one. But I didn't beg him not to do it; I didn't even tell him the truth when he asked if I'd changed my mind. I could have stopped him. I know I could.

If he survives, will he hate me? "Can I see him?" I whisper.

"Not now."

"But he'll be okay?"

"I don't know." She sees the look on my face. "I really don't, Melody. I don't know any more than what I told you."

I nod, and my eyes fill with tears again. "Can I please just go home? My parents will freak out if I'm not home by midnight."

"Curfew?"

I nod. "Uh-huh."

"We can phone them."

"But I don't want them to know about this."

"Melody, you're how old?" She glances down at the sheet of paper in her hand. "Fifteen?"

"Sixteen."

"Don't you think your parents would want to know?"

I don't want to cry. I clench my fists, digging the nails into my palms. "I'll tell them."

She looks at me for a long moment. "I need to make sure that you're safe."

"I am," I tell her. "I wasn't going to jump."

Her dark eyes are steady on mine, and I have to force myself not to look away. "Honestly, I wasn't," I say. "I just— I just never realized that Jeremy was serious about it. And then when I did realize? It was too late."

"Tell me a bit about Jeremy," she says. "How did you two meet, anyway?"

"School, I guess," I tell her. "Right at the beginning of this year. We just started talking."

Death Row

The very first conversation I had with Jeremy was about death. It was back in September, the sky wide open and blue, the sun a hot white disk. I was sitting on the steps of the church across the street from the school, because there's no smoking on school property—and I was reading Camus and rolling a cigarette when he sat down beside me.

"Hey," he said. "Got a light?"

I put my finger in my book to mark my place and squinted up at him. He was tall and very skinny, and pale for post-summer Florida. I didn't know him, but he looked vaguely familiar in a seen-him-around-the-school kind of way. I stuck my hand into my purse, felt around for my lighter and handed it to him.

He lit a cigarette. "I don't usually smoke," he said. "Actually, I just bummed this off someone so I'd have an excuse to talk to you."

I raised my eyebrows. "Yeah, right." Across the street, I could see a group of girls standing close together, laughing and talking. Devika and Adriana and some others. I wondered if they had put him up to this.

"You roll your own, huh? That's kind of cool."

I shrugged. "What do you want?"

"Nothing." He drummed his fingers on his thigh, took a drag on the cigarette and made a face. "Gross. I don't get why anyone smokes."

"Nearly everyone on death row smokes," I said.

He butted out the cigarette. "We're all on death row."

I snorted. "I mean literally. The prisoners at State. They all smoke."

"I meant it literally too. We don't know our execution dates, but we're all under the same sentence."

"What, are you some school shooter or something? Gonna kill everyone?"

He gave a sudden laugh, and it totally changed his face. "No. Jesus, no. I just meant we're all going to die eventually."

"Uh, yeah. Obviously." I looked back at my book. "If you don't mind, I'm actually reading."

"Sure." He stood up. "I'm Jeremy, by the way."

"Melody." I figured he already knew that. "You can tell your friends over there that they can kiss my ass."

"My friends?" He looked in the direction I was pointing, at the cluster of girls in front of the school. "Them? Ah, no. Not my friends."

"Fine," I said. "Mine neither." I opened my book on my lap and tried to read, but he was still standing there and I couldn't concentrate. The heat of the sun was radiating from the cement, and the light reflecting off the page of my book hurt my eyes.

"I'll see you around," he said.

I nodded. I didn't mean to look up at him, but I couldn't help it. My eyes met his, and he didn't look away or blink or smile. He just looked right back at me. It was the weirdest thing, but I felt like he was looking right into me. Like he was actually *seeing* me in a way no one else had ever bothered to.

I dropped my gaze back down to my book, flustered and not wanting him to see the color rising in my cheeks. When I looked up again, he was gone.

≈

The door opens and the gray-haired nurse pokes her head into the small hospital room. "Christine, can I talk to you for a second?"

Christine stands up. "Sure. Just a moment, Melody."

I nod and watch her as she slips out the door, not quite closing it behind her. I strain to listen, but although I can see Christine's back—bright green shirt, black pants—all I can hear is the murmur of their voices. I can't make out the words. I'm glad to have a minute to myself though, to think. To get my story straight. Most of all, I don't want my parents freaking out. I don't want them to think I'm suicidal. They'd be devastated. There's no way to explain what happened.

I'll have to stick with what I told the social worker— that I was trying to talk Jeremy out of jumping. It feels like another betrayal, but I can't see any alternative. Telling the truth is not an option.

The door opens again, and my breath catches in my throat as I see who is entering the room behind Christine.

"Mrs. Weathers," I stammer out. I've only met her once and we didn't say much more than hi. She's tall and thin, like Jeremy, with dark hair and fair skin. She's gorgeous, but right now she looks like hell. Her hair is straggling over her shoulders, and she's wearing saggy-butt track pants and a T-shirt, with a raincoat pulled over top.

"Melody," she says. Her eyes are all red.

I stand up awkwardly. "I'm so sorry," I blurt out. "I should have stopped him."

"You did your best," she says, and she reaches out to pull me into a hug. I put my arms around her and I can feel her shoulders shaking with sobs. "Don't blame yourself."

I pull away. If she knew the truth, she'd hate me.

"Did you know...did he seem depressed to you?" she asks. "I can't believe this. How could he? He seemed *fine*. I've been going over everything in my head, again and again, trying to figure out what I missed."

Christine murmurs something sympathetic, but Mrs. Weathers ignores her. "Did he say anything to you, Melody?" she asks. "Did you know he was thinking about doing something like this?"

I shake my head. "Not really. No. I mean, not before, you know, tonight." My heart is beating so loudly I swear she must hear it, and my palms are slick with sweat.

My mom says she can always tell when I'm lying. She says I'm terrible at hiding things. I hope to god she's wrong about that.

≈

The whole suicide thing had started out as a game. Or maybe not a game, exactly, but a fantasy of sorts. A sort of dark joke, I guess. I wouldn't admit this to anyone— especially now—but it had actually been kind of fun.

It started the second time I talked to Jeremy. After that first meeting across from the school, I started noticing him in the hallways. I'd nod hi and he'd nod back, but we didn't really talk. Then one day I found something jammed into the crack of my locker: a piece of lined paper, folded over and over into a tiny square. I pulled it free. It was one of those things you make as a kid, where you fold the paper to make little pockets and put your thumbs and fingers in to make it open and close like a little paper mouth.

I looked closer. The four corners each had a number on them, one through four. I tried to remember how the game worked. Pick a number, then open and close that many times. One, two, three. Now what? Pick a flap to open? I felt a prickle of irritation. Was this some trick, another *let's mock Melody* moment? I unfolded the toy to see what nasty comments were written inside. There were eight tiny triangles, each with a message neatly written out in minuscule letters.

And they all said the same thing: *"Since we're all going to die, it's obvious that when and how don't matter." (Camus, L'Étranger, 1942) Melody, meet me after school? Let's hang out. From Jeremy, your compatriot on Death Row*   .

I couldn't help grinning. It was weird, but so what? I'd always been pretty weird myself.

Jeremy was waiting for me at the bottom of the steps in front of the school.

"Hey," I said, lifting one hand in a wave.

"Nice nails," he said.

I held them out for his inspection: short and lime green, with pink skull-and-crossbones stickers on them. "Suzy, this kid I babysit, did them for me." Suzy's eight, a third-grader with a genius IQ, an obsession with outer space, a very pink bedroom and questionable fashion sense. "You like?"

"Very, uh, *Pirates of the Caribbean*," he said. "Disney princess meets Jack Sparrow."

I rolled my eyes. "Yeah, that's what I was going for."

Devika and Adriana walked past us, turned and stared over their shoulders for a moment, then started whispering and giggling as if they'd just caught Jeremy and me doing something much more outrageous than having a conversation.

"What's that all about?" Jeremy asked. "How come those girls give you a hard time?"

I liked that about him, the way he was actually interested, the way he asked questions as if he wanted to understand me better—but this was one question I didn't want to answer. "Honestly, you don't know?"

He actually blushed, which was rather endearing in a goofy kind of way. "I heard something, but I didn't know if it was bullshit."

"What did you hear?"

Jeremy hesitated. "I heard you attempted suicide last year. At a party."

I wondered if that was why he'd approached me: curiosity about my supposed suicidal tendencies. "Yeah," I said. "They call me Death Wish. Nice, huh? So supportive."

"Did you, then? I mean, is it true?"

I shook my head. "Not really. I'd had a few drinks and I was all depressed. I took a few Tylenol, like five or six, and stupidly told someone. Adriana. I thought she was a friend." I shrugged and tucked my hands into the long sleeves of my sweater. "Next thing I know, I'm being forced into an ambulance and the whole school knows about it."

"*Five* Tylenol? Huh. Girls always do that. Or else they cut themselves." He grinned. "They like the drama without the real risk."

"I never said I was trying to kill myself. Duh. If I wanted to die, I'd have taken the whole bottle of Tylenol, okay? I'm not an idiot. Smoking, now? I guess that's probably going to kill me if I live long enough."

"So which is it, then? You want to die or not?"

Not, I was about to say, but I didn't want him to lose interest. Besides, sometimes I thought maybe I really did. Sometimes I thought the world seriously sucked. "I don't care enough either way," I told him. "Like it says on my report cards, I'm unmotivated."

He laughed. "Ah, a suicidal underachiever."

I liked his laugh, the clear light sound of it, the way he lifted his chin, the way his eyes narrowed into dark lashed lines.

He leaned back against the brick wall of the school. "When I saw you the first time, you were reading Camus, weren't you? *The Stranger*?"

I raised my eyebrows. "Aren't you observant."

"I wasn't being stalkerish or anything. I always notice what people are reading."

"Have you read it?"

He shook his head. "I started. Couldn't get into it."

"You should try again," I told him.

"Yeah. I just couldn't relate to the character. What's his name again?"

"Meursault."

"Yeah. I mean, at the start of the book, when his mother dies and he's just, you know, like nothing happened? It just seemed a bit out there, you know?"

"Hmm," I said noncommittally. "Haven't you ever not reacted the way people thought you should?"

"Probably. Still."

"I know. It's kind of extreme."

"I've read some of his other stuff. I do better with nonfiction. I'll lend you *The Myth of Sisyphus*, if you like. Did you know that Camus said suicide was the fundamental philosophical question?"

"Did he? What, like to be or not to be?"

"Basically, yeah."

"Shakespeare said it first, then."

He just laughed. "Death Wish," he said. "It's kind of cute, actually. Can I call you DW for short?"

"No," I said. "You can't."

It didn't feel like a particularly important conversation at the time, but I guess that's really where it all began.

Death Penalty

Mrs. Weathers is crying and Christine is talking softly to her, and even though we're all crowded into this tiny room, I think they've both forgotten about me. I'm wondering if I could perhaps slip away when there is another knock on the door.

"Mrs. Weathers?" A doctor—at least, I assume he is, because he's wearing hospital greens—steps into the room. "Jeremy is out of surgery. It went well. He has a number of fractures, several ribs were broken, and he had a collapsed lung." He clears his throat and fingers the name tag that hangs around his neck. "His spleen was ruptured, and we've had to remove it. A couple of fractured vertebrae, but luckily, no spinal cord injury. He's going to be here for quite some time, but there's every reason to believe that he should make a good recovery."

Mrs. Weathers stands up and starts crying harder than ever. "Oh god. Oh, thank you. Thank you. Can I see him?"

The doctor nods. "He's not conscious yet, but you can see him."

She follows him out of the room without a word to me, and I watch her go. I wonder what Jeremy will say when he regains consciousness.

Christine turns back to me. "Well, that's good news."

I try to smile and feel like I'm wearing a mask. "Yes. Yes."

"Amazing, really. After a fall like that. What is it, a hundred feet?"

"Uh, more like a hundred and ninety, I think." I wish I could suck the words back in. I shouldn't know that, should I? I tug at the hem of my short dress, pulling it down toward my knees. My bare thighs look inappropriately naked against the plastic chair.

"A miracle," Christine says.

A miracle. I suppose it is, if you believe in that sort of thing. It's not that I'm not glad he's alive—of course I am. I just can't believe he jumped.

"Let's call your parents," Christine says. "I don't see any reason to keep you here, but I'd feel better about you going home with a responsible adult."

It's not like I can keep this a secret. "I'll call them." I take my phone out of my pocket and dial home.

Vicky picks up on the first ring. "Melody? Where are you?"

"I'm at the hospital. Um, Bayfront Medical Center."

"Oh my god. Are you okay? What's wrong?" Her voice is rising, and I know she's picturing car crashes, drunk drivers, god knows what.

"I'm fine, Vicky. It's Jeremy." And then I lose it, crying so hard that I can't even speak, and Christine gently takes the phone out of my hand and fills Vicky in on all the gory details: *Melody's friend Jeremy...a suicide attempt... seriously injured...*I feel kind of numb, like a part of me is separate and just watching myself fall apart. I can't believe any of this is happening.

I can't understand how I ended up here.

~~~

It is weird how one thing leads to another. I might never have talked to Jeremy if he hadn't noticed the book I was reading. My mom would feel awful if she knew that, because she was the one who gave me the book. She thought I'd be interested, not because of the whole life-is-absurd theme, but because—spoiler alert—the main character gets sentenced to death.

The death penalty is a big deal around here. Florida has more prisoners on death row than any other state, though Texas actually kills more. Everyone knows when there's an execution scheduled. Protesters show up from all over, university students organize stuff, tensions run pretty high. My mother has been an activist since I was a toddler, and she's lost more than a few friends because of it. She's the chair of this local group and she's always doing something—going to meetings, phoning senators and reporters, blogging, circulating online petitions and printing out flyers. My dad, Bill, is a prof at USF and is more academic than practical, but he's against the death penalty too. Which is good, because otherwise they'd probably have had to get a divorce. Despite all her talk about open-mindedness, Vicky can't accept anyone disagreeing with her on this subject.

Bill's brother—my uncle Pete—lives three hours away, in Jacksonville, and works at Florida State Prison. Vicky is always trying to get him on side. Last time was at my sixteenth-birthday dinner.

"You don't have to support the death penalty just because you work there," she told him. "In fact, that's all the more reason to oppose it. You know these men."

Pete rubbed his short beard. "They've done some horrible things, Vicky. Maybe they deserve to die."

"And who are we to judge that?" My mother's voice was calm. "Most of them have horrific backgrounds. Childhood abuse. Poverty. They are who they are for a reason, Pete."

"We all make choices," Pete said. "They made bad ones." He never seems to mind Mom arguing with him. He's pretty unflappable.

"Doesn't it bother you?" I asked him. "Getting to know someone, taking care of them, sort of, and knowing that they're going to be killed?"

He shrugged. "Be worse if no one took care of them. Someone's gotta do it." He cut himself a second slice of key lime pie, pulled out the birthday candle and licked it. "Mmm. Vicky, this pie is to die for."

I put down my fork, thinking about the men who'd been executed at the state prison over the last year. Vicky had their pictures up on the wall in her office. "Still," I said. "It seems kind of…I don't know, cold-blooded. Keeping them alive for years and then killing them."

"Better than killing them right away," he said. "They get their due legal process and all that. Besides, half these guys have appeals pending; they could be around for years."

Vicky just shook her head. It was a conversation they had been having for years, and as far as I could see, it was a waste of her time. Pete wasn't going to change his mind. When he and I were alone together, he'd tell me all kinds of stories about the men on death row, and sometimes I felt like I knew them.

There's a lot of stuff that bothers me about death row, but it's the details that get to me the most. Like the whole deal of the prisoners requesting a last meal. Before Pete started working there, I always figured that last-meal business was just in the movies, but they actually do it. It seems so weird to prepare some fancy dish and then, the next day, kill the guy who ate it.

Rennie, the last guy, asked for a chocolate shake, a cheeseburger and fries. He was forty-five and had been on death row for fifteen years. He killed a convenience-store clerk in a robbery when he was in his late twenties, which is horrible, but by the time they executed him, he'd converted to Catholicism and earned a history degree. That's who they killed—not the young guy who killed the clerk. I mean, what's the point? How does that make any sense at all?

Anyway, Vicky's been fighting against the death penalty for as long as I can remember. Before I was born, she was a social worker in child protection. Then, when she was on mat leave, she got involved with an advocacy group, and by the time I was starting preschool, she was running it. She had a job too—counseling families and running support groups for parents—but her volunteer work was her real passion. It was weird: most people didn't think much about the people living on death row, but I felt like I'd grown up with this huge extended family of people all waiting to die. I could date events in my life by who was executed that year.

I didn't usually get into my mom's business with kids at school, but a couple of weeks after we started hanging out, Jeremy told me he wanted to meet my parents.

Why? I typed. It was late, and I was in bed; we were texting.

Why not? I'm always curious about people's families.

Huh, I typed back. Brilliant. Could I be any less eloquent? God.

It's interesting, don't u think?

I hadn't really thought much about it.

You get along with your folks ok?

Yes. You?

Complicated. What do yours do?

I rolled over on my bed, balancing my phone on my pillow. Dad's a prof. Mom does counseling and volunteers a lot. No need to get into that now. Yours?

Teachers. Divorced. High school. Math and English. Different schools. So when can I come over?

I've never been one of those kids who gets embarrassed by their parents. I love Vicky and Bill, and even though they make me crazy at times, I actually have a lot of respect for them both. So I wasn't quite sure why I didn't want to introduce Jeremy to them. I sighed in the darkness. He wasn't going to drop it. After school tomorrow? I typed.

≈

The next day, Jeremy and I headed back to my place together after school. It just felt easy being with him, like we'd known each other for a long time. I wondered if he had a girlfriend. I'd never seen him with anyone. Maybe he was gay.

I glanced sideways at him as we rounded the corner onto my street. Halloween was a week away, and there were pumpkins everywhere, and those Kleenex ghosts hanging from the trees.

"Wow. Your neighborhood really gets into Halloween, huh?"

My family lives in Old Northeast. It's one of my favorite parts of St. Petersburg, the kind of neighborhood where people hang out on their front porches, wave to the joggers and dog walkers, and look for any excuse for a community celebration. "Just wait," I said. "Some of these folks have barely gotten started." I pointed at a narrow wood-shingled house with two very crooked palm trees in front of it. "That house there? There's these two gay men who live there—some kind of artists, I think, but they're in, like, their eighties—and they do a haunted-house setup you won't believe." I stopped walking and looked at Jeremy. "Hey, are you doing anything for Halloween?"

He shook his head. "No plans. I usually stay home. Actually, it's kind of goofy, but I love handing out candy."

"We should go trick-or-treating," I said. "Old Northeast is awesome for trick-or-treating. We even close the streets for the evening."

He laughed. "I haven't been since I was about eleven."

"Yeah, same. Maybe twelve. I think I was a vampire. You?"

"Um, one of the Blues Brothers. Hat, sunglasses and sideburns."

"God, weren't you original."

"Yeah, that's me." He made a face. "That costume was my mom's idea. The year before, I was a pepper shaker."

He sounded sort of bitter, and a frown creased his forehead. I wondered what was wrong. "Come on," I said. "Let's do something."

"Maybe." He sounded reluctant.

"Okay, not trick-or-treating. But we could make something cool for the kids, like a graveyard kind of thing. Then you'd still get to hand out candy."

Jeremy shook his head. "We'll see. Let me talk to my mom, okay? She might want me to stay home."

"This is my place," I said, pointing.

He stared. "No way. You did those?"

I nodded. "Yup." A row of carved pumpkins, more than a dozen of them, sat grinning and leering and frowning along the front path. We did it every year, me and Vicky and Bill, and this year, Suzy too. It had become kind of a tradition, and I loved it.

"Awesome."

We walked along the path and I pointed at a big pumpkin perched on the bottom step. "That's my best one. You like it?" I'd carved a cat, back arched, against a background of a full moon and a tombstone.

"That's amazing. How d'you do that?"

I grinned. "I drew it on paper first, made a stencil. Then you just scrape off the skin and keep scraping until the pumpkin shell is really thin, so the light glows through where the moon is, and the cat's like a silhouette. It looks really cool when it's lit."

"Wow." He studied the pumpkin for a long moment, then looked up at the front steps, at the red front door and the gray wooden porch. "Nice house."

"Come on in," I said.

Another Chance

Vicky was working at the computer, which lives in a corner of the living room, but she swiveled her chair around when she heard us.

"Mel?" She tucked her short brown hair behind her ears and looked from me to Jeremy.

"Hi, Vicky. This is Jeremy."

"Hi. Just let me save this…" She turned back to the screen, clicked a few keys and stood up. "Nice to meet you, Jeremy. You guys want a drink or something? I've just made a pot of coffee; it's probably ready."

"Coffee would be great," I said. I've been a coffee drinker since I was about eight. It used to horrify my friends' parents that Vicky and Bill let me drink coffee, but it didn't seem to have done me any harm. We only ever had decaf anyway.

We all headed into the kitchen. Vicky pulled three mugs out of the dishwasher and poured coffee into them while I got milk out of the fridge.

"None of us take sugar, so we never have a sugar bowl," I apologized. I heaved a five-pound bag of sugar out of the baking cupboard. "So if you take sugar..."

Jeremy grinned. "Yeah, that should be enough."

"So you two are at school together?" Vicky asked.

I nodded. "Yup."

"You're a sophomore too?"

"Junior," Jeremy said, and we carried our mugs over to the kitchen table and sat down.

"Do you have any brothers or sisters, Jeremy?" Vicky asked. She could talk to anyone easily. She'd told me that she used to be shy, and that she still considered herself an introvert, but she sure knew how to put people at ease and strike up a conversation. Unlike me.

But Jeremy suddenly went quiet. He stirred sugar into his coffee, slowly and deliberately. "Um. No. No, I don't."

"An only child, like Melody," Vicky said. "I am too, actually. Funny, when I was a kid that seemed so unusual. But I guess big families are the exception these days."

"I had a brother," Jeremy said abruptly. "Lucas. He died two years ago."

I stared at him, my mouth hanging open.

Vicky stopped wiping the counter and sat down at the kitchen table with us. "I'm so sorry, Jeremy."

There was a silence, and I wondered if Vicky was

going to ask how he died. I wanted to know, but I wasn't about to ask.

"Had he been ill?" she asked. "Or was it an accident?"

"He drowned," Jeremy said. "At St. Pete Beach."

Vicky closed her eyes for a second, and when she reopened them, they were shining ever so slightly. I hoped she wasn't going to cry. "How awful," she said. "It's every parent's worst nightmare, I think, losing a child. I am so sorry, Jeremy. How old was he?"

"Thirteen." Jeremy shrugged. "It was awful, but…well, it was two years ago. I'm okay, Mrs.—"

"Vicky. Call me Vicky." She stood up again, taking the hint. "Well, can you stay for dinner, Jeremy? Bill should be home soon—or not. His schedule's a bit unpredictable."

I gave a snort. "He doesn't have a schedule. It's his work habits that are unpredictable."

Vicky laughed ruefully. "That's true, I'm afraid. Sometimes he stays at the university until midnight, working on a paper. Other times he's home so much you'd swear the man was unemployed."

"I'd love to stay for dinner." Jeremy gave her a particularly charming smile, and I thought to myself that he could be an actor, or a politician. This was a side of him I'd never seen before. Not phony, exactly, just kind of polished. "So what about you, Vicky? Mel mentioned that you do a lot of volunteer work."

Vicky looked at me, eyebrows raised slightly. She knew I generally avoided bringing up the subject of her work, having had a few too many arguments about the topic. "I run an advocacy group. We petition against the death penalty."

"Cool." Jeremy grinned at me, and I felt a flicker of nervousness. It suddenly seemed important to me that my mother liked him. That she didn't think he was too smooth or that he was kissing up.

"You don't have to agree just because she's my mother," I said irritably. "Vicky can handle an argument, believe me."

Vicky looked at me, eyebrows raised, but didn't say anything.

"Actually, I do agree," Jeremy said. He was looking at my mother, not at me. "I mean, I don't know what I think about the death penalty. I go back and forth, to be honest. But I think it's cool that you do that. Most people just complain about things but don't do anything."

Vicky smiled at him. "Well, a lot of what we do could probably be described as complaining. We're trying to present a strong, unified voice to oppose state-sanctioned cold-blooded killing."

"That's the thing, isn't it?" Jeremy said. "I mean, it's disturbing that it is planned and deliberate and cold-blooded, but it'd be worse if it wasn't. I mean, if it was impulsive? If the government had executioners who killed people in a rage? Or, you know, vigilantes who took the law into their own hands?"

"Either way, people are killed," Vicky said. "And some of them are innocent."

"What about the ones who are for sure guilty?" Jeremy asked. "I mean, say there's a ton of witnesses? Or what if it's a totally horrific kind of crime? Kidnapping and torturing and killing a kid, for example. Videotaped evidence, no shred of a doubt. Do you ever think that maybe some people really do deserve the death penalty?"

Vicky shook her head, and I braced myself for a speech I'd heard at least a thousand times. "I don't think we understand what makes people do the things they do. Almost everyone who ends up on death row comes from a pretty rough background."

"Tell him about what you used to do," I said. "You know. The court stuff."

"You can tell him yourself," she said.

"No, you'll explain it better."

Vicky's expression hovered between amused and annoyed, but she turned to Jeremy. "When Mel was little, I used to do assessments in death-penalty cases. Getting their family history, documenting abuse they'd experienced, their exposure to traumatic events. Looking for mitigating factors that could be used to argue for a reduced sentence. And every single one, without exception, had survived truly horrible things. Child abuse, poverty, neglect. Some of them were born already damaged by fetal alcohol syndrome and then abused by their families and betrayed by the foster-care system. Yes, some of them have done terrible things, but there's a reason they became who they are." She paused, looked Jeremy in the eye. "And it's the same society that has let them down that then kills them."

"But aren't they still responsible for their actions?" Jeremy argued. "I mean, not everyone who has a bad childhood becomes a murderer."

Vicky nodded. "Sure, lots of people overcome their pasts. But when you look at these men's histories—a few women too—it's hard to argue that the responsibility for their actions lies with them alone."

The front door opened and I heard Bill kicking off his shoes. I mean that literally: he wears these slip-on shoes that most people would only wear for gardening, and when he comes home he kicks them ten feet down the hall and tries to land them in this wicker basket that was originally meant for the cat.

"Hi, honey," Vicky called out.

Bill wandered into the room, a file folder under one arm and a book in his hand. He's such a stereotype of the absent-minded professor, right down to the corduroy jacket and suede elbow patches. Bill was one of those genius kids—he started university at fourteen, graduated at seventeen, had a doctorate by twenty-one— and he told me once that he had deliberately cultivated a certain image because he wanted to be taken seriously. He even used to smoke a pipe, but he gave that up before I was born, thank god. The jackets he kept, because they were comfortable and because he hated shopping.

He claims that he doesn't care about image anymore. *Just be yourself, Mel. Don't waste your energy worrying about what other people think*, he always says. Nice idea, if you could just switch that kind of thing on and off.

"Bill, this is my friend Jeremy," I told him.

He put the folder and the book down on the kitchen counter and looked at me, then at Jeremy. "Nice to meet you, Jeremy."

"Nice to meet you too, Mr.—"

"Bill." He nodded distractedly at Jeremy, then turned to face Vicky. "You won't believe what they decided at the faculty meeting today. Unbelievable."

Jeremy looked at me, and I rolled my eyes. "Want to see my room?"

"Sure." He stood and followed me up the stairs and through the door at the top. Then he stopped, staring. "Wow."

Basically, I have the whole upstairs to myself, except for one small space, which we call the spare room but which is really more like a storage unit. Our house is almost a hundred years old but totally not heritage, since every inch of it has been redone. My room is huge and open concept: two bedrooms knocked into one by the people who owned the house before us. One end is set up like a living room, with a couch and TV and PS3; the other end has my bed and dresser and a walk-in closet. There's a bathroom right off the bedroom, and skylights over my bed.

"This is your room? You have your own freaking apartment?"

"Pretty much."

"Unbelievable." Jeremy ran his hand along the shelf of PS3 games. "You're a gamer? I wouldn't have guessed that."

"Not so much anymore. From eleven to thirteen or so, it was pretty much all I did. I guess the interest kind of burned itself out though."

He picked up one case. "Huh. A LEGO Harry Potter game?"

I took it out of his hand and put it back on the shelf. "Like I said, I was eleven."

He grinned at me. "So where do your parents sleep?"

"Downstairs. Their bedroom is what would normally be the family room or den or whatever. It's got a fireplace. It's nice." I could hear myself sounding defensive. "It was their choice, okay? It's not like I kicked them out of their room or anything, okay? We moved here four years ago, and my parents said I was old enough to need my own space."

"Wow."

I flopped down on the couch. "I know. Vicky and Bill are cool."

"How come you call them that? Instead of Mom and Dad?"

"Dunno. Always have done." It seems strange to me that most people don't use their parents' names. I can't imagine calling Vicky *Mom*. It would be like her calling me *Daughter* or calling Bill *Husband*.

"Weird," he said. "My mother wouldn't go for that."

"Families are different." I shrugged, and there was a long silence. Finally, I cleared my throat. "So, hey, I never knew about your brother."

"Yeah, well."

"How come you never told me?"

"Never came up."

"Yeah, 'cause you never brought it up." I sat up straighter and tucked my feet under my butt.

Jeremy sat a couple of feet away, perched on the arm of the couch. "It's kind of a hard thing to work into a conversation. Like, yeah, so did I ever tell you about the time my brother drowned?"

"Seemed easy enough to tell my mother," I said. I knew I was being stupid, but I couldn't seem to stop myself.

"She's pretty awesome."

"Yeah."

"What does that mean? You don't think so?"

"No, I do." I chipped at the nail polish on my thumb, flaking it off in bright, shiny scales. "She's great. They both are."

"You look like your mom, you know."

"You think?" I guess I do, sort of. We both have thick blondish-brown hair—hers is shorter and blonder, because she gets it highlighted—and brown eyes. She's taller, though, and curvier, and more stylish. I looked like a boy until I was twelve, and still would if I cut my hair and wore a baggy sweatshirt.

"You totally do. Anyway, she's cool. You're lucky. I mean, seriously."

"I *know*. Jesus, Jeremy. Enough already."

He raised his eyebrows and leaned away from me exaggeratedly. "Whoa. Okay, what's wrong?"

I shook my head. "Nothing. Just, you know, sometimes…"

"They're not as perfect as they seem?"

"No. They are. Well, not perfect, I guess, but they're pretty great. It's just that sometimes it's a lot to live up to. You know? Like, I feel guilty if I'm not perfectly happy and confident and…I don't know. I just don't want to let them down."

Jeremy frowned. "I bet they wouldn't see it that way."

I rolled my eyes. "Of course they wouldn't. They'd be sympathetic and understanding and they'd tell me for the gazillionth time how much they love me and believe in me." I sniffled, unexpected tears prickling my eyes. "Just... sometimes I think they see me as better than I really am. That's all."

He didn't say anything for a long moment. Then he reached out and took my hand between his. "Poor little rich girl," he said, mocking but gentle.

"We're not rich," I said automatically.

He looked around my room, eyebrows raised, and I felt my cheeks get warm. "I didn't mean money," he said.

I pulled my hand away. "You totally changed the subject."

"I did? What were we talking about?"

I narrowed my eyes at him. "Your brother."

"Lucas."

Jeremy was six feet to my five four, and his perch on the arm of the couch made him even taller. I had to lean back and look up to meet his eyes. "Tell me about him."

"He was two years younger than me," he said. "He'd have turned fifteen this month."

"Mmm." I wondered if I'd been with Jeremy on Lucas's birthday. If he'd been thinking about him and hadn't said a word to me. "What was he like?"

"Mr. Normal, you know? Everyone liked him. Teachers, other kids. He was smart but not freaky smart. Good soccer player. Getting into skateboarding." He nodded at my shelf of games. "Spent a lot of quality time with his Xbox."

"Were you guys close?"

He shook his head. "When we were younger, I guess we were. Not so much in the last couple of years." He gave a short laugh. "I was too weird for him."

"Freaky smart?"

"Just freaky, I guess." Jeremy made a face. "He figured I'd be bad for his reputation when he got to high school."

Only he never did get to high school. "What happened?" I asked. "I mean, if you don't want to talk about it, that's okay. I just wondered."

"How he died, you mean?" His mouth twisted mockingly. "People always want to know that."

"I didn't mean to be nosy," I said.

"Human nature." Jeremy was silent for a moment. "What do you believe, Mel? About death, I mean."

I stuck my fingertip between my teeth and bit down on the nail. Bad habit. The thing is, what I believe didn't seem like it'd be much comfort to someone whose brother was dead. "Um, I'm not religious or anything," I said lamely. "So I don't know. I mean, you can't really know, can you?"

"I believe we come back."

"Like reincarnation?"

"Yes. I think life and death are a cycle. A wheel, you know?" He made a circling gesture with one hand.

"You think Lucas has been reborn?" I said, trying to sound neutral.

"Or will be. Yeah."

"Huh." I tried to remember what little I knew about reincarnation. "Um, as a person? I mean, you know…"

"Not as a cat or a bug? Yeah, as a person. I don't buy the whole hierarchy thing, where you move up if you're good and down if you're bad. That's just social control, right?"

"Like heaven and hell," I said. "Gives people a reason to behave themselves."

He looked at me for a long moment. "I don't think murderers come back as cockroaches or anything, but I do think it makes a difference, what we do in this life. That's what I don't like about the whole heaven and hell idea. It gets people all focused on some afterlife, as if that's what's important. But with reincarnation, we just come back to this same world. So whatever we do, the effect we have in the world, it all matters."

I nodded.

"And it means you get another chance," he said. "To do things right. So in my next life, I'll take better care of Lucas." He gave a short laugh. "Because I sure fucked that up this time around."

≈

That evening, after Jeremy went home, I had a weird conversation with Vicky. I was brushing my teeth when she knocked on my bathroom door. "Mel?"

"Come in."

She walked into my bathroom. "Getting ready for bed?"

I nodded and spoke through a mouthful of toothpaste. "Tired."

She opened my medicine cabinet. "Think I'm getting a cold. Do you have any vitamin C?"

I spat in the sink. "Don't think so. Thought you said that was an urban myth anyway."

She made a face. "Yeah, well, there's not much evidence that it works, but it's harmless, right? And I can't afford to get sick right now."

"Busy?"

"Yeah. Ramon is coming up for his last appeal, and it doesn't look good."

I stuck my toothbrush back in the holder. "Mmm."

She followed me out of the bathroom. "Mel, I was wondering…is Jeremy someone important to you?"

"Sure, I guess."

"I don't mean to pry," she said. "I just wondered."

"I haven't known him that long," I said. "We just kind of clicked though. He's a good friend."

"Just a friend?"

"I'm not sleeping with him, if that's what you mean." Something else occurred to me. "Tell me you weren't checking my medicine cabinet for birth control."

Her cheeks flared, red and blotchy. "I'm sorry. That was...I shouldn't have done that. I just wanted to say, if you want to go on the pill...or to talk about options..."

I held up a hand to stop her. "Not. Sleeping. With. Jeremy." I made a face. "Or anyone else, for that matter. And don't worry: if I was going to, I wouldn't be stupid about it."

"I know you wouldn't."

I raised my eyebrows at her.

"Okay, okay. Sorry. I *should* know you wouldn't. But he's older than you, right?"

"Not by much—"

"And I remember being your age, Mel. I know how fast things can happen. How fast things can get out of control."

"Yeah, well, not in my life, okay?"

"Okay."

"So, did you like him?" I asked, just to change the subject a little.

"He was very polite." She hesitated. "And he seems bright."

"Yeah, he is." I sat down on the edge of my bed. "How come you didn't answer the question?"

"Mel, I don't know him." She looked uncomfortable.

"You didn't like him, did you?" I glared at her, trying to read between her words. "Why not?"

"I didn't say that. Don't twist my words."

"Do you know his mom or something? Is she in one of your Parents Talking with Teens groups?"

Vicky frowned. "I couldn't tell you if she was; you know that. But no, I haven't met his parents."

"Then why are you being all weird about him? Because you thought I was sleeping with him? Is that it?"

"No. I don't know. Maybe." She gestured helplessly. "Look, Mel, we've always been able to talk about things, right? But you're sixteen; you're entitled to your own life and your privacy. And you make your own choices about friendships and who to trust."

"Gosh, thanks."

"Don't be sarcastic," she said. "Like I said, I don't even know Jeremy. I just felt...concerned. About him. Not you."

"Because of his brother?"

46

"Maybe, yeah. That threw me."

"Me too."

"You didn't know?"

"Nope."

"How did he drown? Did he tell you?"

I realized he hadn't. I'd asked, but he'd started talking about reincarnation instead of answering. "Not really," I said.

She nodded. "Maybe it's all those years as a counselor, Mel. But I just get the feeling there's more to Jeremy than meets the eye."

"Isn't that a good thing? I hate shallow people."

"I know. But it's hard to know what's hiding in the depths sometimes." She sighed. "And I'm your mother; I worry, okay? Can't help it."

"Well, don't." I stood up and gave her a hug. "I'm fine. He's a friend. And if I ever want to go on the pill, you can take me to see Dr. Rosewater, okay? You can hold my hand in the waiting room."

She laughed. "You're making fun of me."

"Yes," I said. "I am. And now I'm kicking you out, because I'm going to bed."

"I love you, Mel. Forever and always. Remember that." Vicky kissed my cheek, my nose, my other cheek. "Sleep tight, love."

"Love you too," I said.

Dreaming

The next day, Jeremy and I hung out at lunch. It was sunny, but in a hazy, humid kind of way that made me feel both tired and restless.

"Wish I had a car," he said. "We could drive somewhere. To St. Pete Beach, maybe. I haven't been there in ages."

We were sitting under a huge mossy oak tree at the far edge of the baseball pitch behind the school. "Isn't that…I mean, I would've thought…"

"My brother?"

I nodded.

"He'll be dead whether I go to the beach or not," he said.

"I know. I just thought it might be hard to go there. For you. Um, like a reminder, you know?"

He snorted. "Hardly something I can forget, Mel."

My cheeks flushed with heat, and I dropped my gaze. I wondered again what had happened. Had Jeremy been there? Did he blame himself for Lucas's drowning? I couldn't imagine asking him.

"You know anything about lucid dreaming?" Jeremy said abruptly.

I shook my head. "Uh, no. Not a thing. Should I?"

"Yeah, actually. It's pretty cool."

"Lucid. Like clear? Vivid?"

"More like aware. You know you're dreaming." He shrugged like it was no big deal, but his eyes were even more intense than usual, holding my gaze so tightly I wanted to squirm. "I've been working at it for the last year," he said. "Really hard."

"Working at dreaming?" I laughed. "What, you sleep a lot? I hate to break it to you, but that doesn't really qualify as hard work."

He didn't even crack a grin. "The first time it happened was an accident. I was asleep and dreaming that I was walking down a hallway." He broke off. "I know other people's dreams are dead boring to listen to, but stay with me, okay?"

I nodded. "All ears."

"So I was walking down a hallway and there were all these doors…"

"Uh-huh."

"And then I thought, hey, this is a dream. Like I woke up, only I was still there in the hallway. It was—I don't know. I was going to say it was weird, but it actually felt really natural."

"So what happened?" I asked.

"I thought, I can choose to open one of these doors. And I'll see the beach behind it. So I opened a door, and sure enough, the beach."

"So you kind of influenced the dream?"

He ignored my question and kept talking, the words coming out fast, as if they were under pressure. "And I thought, Lucas is here. And my heart was racing so fast. I ran along the sand…and I caught a glimpse of him. He was standing right there. I could see the ocean behind him. I could smell it." He shook his head and blew out a long breath. "And then I woke up. But it was so real. Even days later, I remembered it so clearly. It didn't fade like dreams usually do. So I started reading about dreams and realized it was what's called a lucid dream."

"Because you knew you were dreaming?"

"Right. So I wanted to make it happen again."

"You can do that?" I frowned. "How? I mean, if you have to be asleep for it to happen…"

"That's why it's so hard."

"Right." I wanted to laugh, but he looked so serious that I didn't dare. "So how do you do it?"

"You have to trick your own brain," he said. "So you start when you're awake. All the time, you ask yourself,

Is this real? Am I dreaming? Like, it starts to rain and you say, Is it really raining? Is this a dream?"

"Weird," I said.

Jeremy leaned forward and his eyes burned into me, coal dark and shadowed. "You have to blur the boundaries," he said. "Awake and asleep. Real and dreaming. You can move in and out of a dream without waking. You can decide what will happen in the dream. Influence how the dream goes as if you are writing a story."

"Would've been useful when I was about eight," I said. "I used to have wicked nightmares." I did too: stupid dreams about being chased by Elmo. A psycho Elmo with eyes like that Chucky doll. I'd wake up screaming and Vicky would come running in and ask what the nightmare was about. I never told her. I was too embarrassed.

"I'll send you some links," he said. "You should try it." He lay down on his back and closed his eyes. His cheeks looked as silky smooth as a child's, not a trace of stubble, and his eyelids were traced with blue veins. His dark hair, usually brushed forward and half hiding his face, had fallen back, exposing his high forehead, and he looked oddly vulnerable. My heart was suddenly beating faster, and I had an awful urge to reach out and stroke his hair.

I started rolling a cigarette instead.

His eyes opened. "Melody. Why do you smoke?"

"I dunno. I don't much. Like, this pack will last me a week." Three a day, max, but Vicky and Bill would be so upset if they knew. I felt guilty every time I thought about that.

"When did you start?"

I sighed. "Last year, start of high school. I was put in the early college prep program, you know?"

He raised his eyebrows. "Really. You don't strike me as the type."

"What, not that smart?"

"Don't be stupid. Of course you're smart. I meant not that much of an ass kisser."

I shrugged. "I wasn't a straight-A student or anything."

"What's this got to do with smoking?"

"Promise you won't laugh?"

He nodded. "Promise."

"So, Devika and Adriana, they didn't get in. And all of a sudden, it was like the fact that we'd been hanging out for two years meant nothing at all. They were making all these cracks about me, saying I was a brownnoser, telling other people that I thought I was better than them…"

"Okay." He looked puzzled but didn't say anything more.

I sighed. "I guess I was just trying to show them I didn't care, you know? Acting all tough and cool. Dressing differently. Smoking. I was trying for a certain image. Dumb, I know."

"Still?" He gestured at my jeans and T-shirt.

"No. It lasted maybe a month. Black clothes, heavy eyeliner, vaguely goth."

He laughed. "Sorry. I just can't see it."

"No, I know. You're right. I couldn't pull it off. I looked like, I don't know, geek girl in goth drag." I broke off, remembering. "That stupid party you heard about…"

"Death Wish?"

"Mmm. That was the end of it. Devika and Adriana were there and I was…I don't know. It was lame. I'd had a few drinks, and I missed hanging out with them. And I took a couple of Tylenol because I had a headache, and then I just had this impulse…I took a couple more, and a couple more. Then I started crying and told Adriana. I guess I wanted her to feel sorry for me or something."

"Maybe she did the right thing, calling an ambulance."

I snorted.

"Seriously. She had no way of knowing how much you'd actually taken. Maybe she was scared."

"She told everyone, Jeremy. I mean, when I came back to school, it was a nightmare." I lit my cigarette. "*Death Wish*."

"Yeah, I know. I heard the stories."

"Is that why you started talking to me? Because of what you'd heard?"

"Maybe." His face was unreadable. "So, you're still in the early college prep program?"

I nodded.

"And you still smoke."

"I like it." I lay down beside him and stared up at the sun. "Watch this." I blew a perfect smoke ring. "See that? It's a lost art."

"A lost art that'll give you cancer."

"I know, duh." I made a face. "I'm going to stop."

"The first time I met you, you said you smoked because everyone on death row smoked."

"They do." I rolled onto my side to face him. We were lying side by side, angled so our heads were only a foot apart. "It's part of the culture."

"Have you been to the prison? I mean, how do you know that?"

"Look online," I said. "There's this woman my mom knows—Pam. She's a graphic designer or something, but she volunteers with Vicky's group. She makes web pages for the inmates. They send her stuff—artwork, stuff they've written, pictures their grandkids send them—and she posts it for them."

"No way."

"Sure, why not?"

He shrugged. "Just seems weird, that's all, to think of them having grandkids."

"They're just people, Jeremy. It seems weird because we don't think of them as people. Because it's easier to kill them if we believe they're monsters. That's why Vicky and

Pam do the website thing. WaitingToDie.com. To show the public their human faces."

"Does anyone actually look at the site?" He sounded doubtful.

"Not so much. People don't want to know." I propped my chin on my elbow. "You want to know what it's like in there? You get three meals a day: five AM, eleven AM and four PM. You eat with a spork. You know that you are going to be killed, but you don't know when. It could be years—"

Jeremy interrupted me. "Mel. It's not your fault they're in there."

"I know." I glared at him. "Obviously."

"You sound angry. What's up?"

I flopped onto my back. "I don't know. I just think about it a lot. That's all." I ground my cigarette out on the grass beside me. "You know the last-meal thing?"

"Uh-huh."

"What would you ask for?"

"I don't know. Um, steak, maybe. Or lobster. Crab legs. And a bottle of red wine. Really good chocolate. Or cheesecake, maybe."

"No can do. Forty bucks. That's the spending limit."

"Okay, skip the lobster..." He trailed off. "For real?"

"For real. And the ingredients all have to be available locally. And it gets cooked by the regular staff, so don't expect miracles." I scowled. "My uncle works at a prison."

"As a guard?"

"No. Something administrative."

"Huh."

Neither of us said anything for a long moment, and I was suddenly acutely conscious of how close his face was to mine. We'd only known each other for a few weeks, but he'd become my best friend. And friends had never come easily to me. I didn't want anything to mess it up. My heart was beating a little faster than it should be. *I'm not attracted to him,* I told myself sternly. *We're friends. That's all.*

I sat up, crossed my legs, folded my arms across my chest. "I'm starving," I said. "Got any food?"

Planning to Die

Vicky and Bill arrive at the hospital faster than I would have thought possible. They look like they just got out of bed—Vicky's hair is flattened on one side, sticking up on the other, and she's wearing a sweatshirt and flannel pants; Bill is bleary-eyed and bewildered-looking. "Melody," Vicky says, and her arms are already around me.

I start to sob again, pushing my head against her shoulder.

"Oh, honey. Oh, honey. I'm so sorry." She rubs my back. "Have you heard how he's doing?"

"He's out of surgery," Christine says. "He's stable. He'll be here for a while though, from the sound of it."

"His mom's here," I whisper. "I saw her."

"Oh, honey," Vicky says again. "What happened? Were you there with him?"

"I didn't think he'd really do it," I say. "I didn't think he'd jump."

"Melody tried to stop him," Christine says. "The police officer said she was right there with him, trying to hold on to him when he jumped."

Vicky pulls back so she can look at me, but I can't meet her eyes. I can't.

"Melody," she says. "Oh, Melody."

And I wonder if she knows. I wonder how much of the truth she guesses.

≈

The plan began almost as a joke. Not a ha-ha kind of joke, more of a black-humor kind of thing. I'd had a crappy day—I can't even remember why. Probably a B on a paper I'd actually worked hard on, or a *Very disappointing* comment from a teacher, or just more hallway stares and whispers than usual. Whatever the reason, I was feeling lousy by the time Jeremy and I met up under our tree.

"Look at you," he said. He was lying on his side on the grass, leaning on an elbow, chin propped on his hand. "Your dog just die?"

"There is no Dog," I said.

"Ha-ha. Come on, what's wrong?"

"Life just sucks sometimes, that's all."

"Ain't that the truth."

And this part I remember as clear as if I'm watching it in high definition. Because Jeremy reached out his arms and pulled me in close, so that I was lying down beside him with my head resting on his chest. I could hear his heart beating and smell the fabric softener on his shirt. He stroked my short hair with one hand, his fingers cool on the back of my neck.

"If things get too bad, we can always check out, right? Like Camus said, the when and how don't matter."

I squeezed my eyes tightly shut. "Yeah. We'll jump off the Skyway Bridge together."

"What'll you have for your last meal?"

I moved one of my hands so that my palm was open against the flatness of his chest. "Mmm. Macaroni and cheese. Onion rings. Root beer. Ice cream."

"You're eating local, all right."

I laughed. "And you?"

"That sounds good to me," he said.

I closed my eyes and just lay there, smiling, wondering what this meant. Where things were going between us. I wasn't thinking about falling from a bridge.

I was too busy wondering whether I was falling in love with my best friend.

≈

Over the next few days, Jeremy and I fell into a pattern of meeting up before school, spending our lunch hours together, coming back to my place after school. He stayed for dinner the next night, and the next, and my parents didn't seem to mind. Sometimes I caught Vicky watching him with a thoughtful sort of look on her face, and I figured she was wondering what was going on between us. I was wondering too. Because although we spent most of our free time together and texted each other whenever we were apart, although everyone at school assumed we were an item, although we often sat snuggled up together like kittens, nothing had actually happened between us.

He treated me like I was his sister.

One evening up in my room, when we'd been playing a game on my PS3, he put down his controller and stretched out on the couch with his head in my lap. I studied his face in the glow of the screen. "Jeremy?"

"Mmm." He didn't open his eyes. I could see the faint blue of veins in his closed eyelids, and his lashes dark as soot against his pale skin. I couldn't decide if he was good-looking or not. His nose was too big, bony and arched. Beaky. His hair and eyebrows were black, his skin very pale and a bit broken out along his jawline, and he was really skinny. Practically skeletal. I could see his collarbones jutting out above his V-neck sweater. If he were a girl, everyone would think he had an eating disorder. He had a nice mouth though, with full lips and straight white teeth.

"What are you thinking about?" I asked him.

"Music."

"What music?"

He opened his eyes and looked at me. "I made this playlist over the summer. You'd like it, Death Wish."

"Don't call me that," I said automatically.

He laughed. "My suicide playlist. I used to think that if I was going to kill myself, I'd do the car-in-garage thing. Carbon monoxide. So this was the music I wanted to listen to on the way out."

"What was on it?"

"It keeps changing. 'How to Disappear Completely' by Radiohead. Frank Ocean's 'Swim Good.' One by Forever the Sickest Kids called 'What Happened to Emotion?'—you know it?"

I nodded. "What else?"

"Um, that old Clash song 'Lose this Skin.' I love that one. And 'Hindsight,' by Death Cab for Cutie. 'Too Far Down,' by Hüsker Dü. Um, a couple from The Used. Lots more. Velvet Underground. I'll send it to you, if you like."

"Well," I said, "that's not going to work so well if we're jumping off the bridge. You better pick a short song."

He laughed. "Maybe we could listen to it over our last meal."

"I want some old stuff on it," I said. "Jazz and blues stuff."

I thought it was all a joke. But who's going to believe that now?

≈

The room at the hospital smells like antiseptic, and I can hear a kid wailing somewhere. Vicky holds my chin lightly in her hand so that I can't look away. "Tell me the truth," she says. "Were you going to jump too?"

"No," I say. "Vicky! No. Of course not." But it's not the whole truth, and I know she can tell.

She looks past me, at Christine. "I don't know if Mel told you, but there was…there was an incident last year. She took some Tylenol…"

"That's not fair," I say. "It has nothing to do with this."

Christine is looking at me now, frowning.

"It wasn't a suicide attempt," I say.

"I didn't say it was," Vicky says carefully. "I just thought that perhaps…"

"It has absolutely nothing to do with this," I say. "It has nothing to do with anything."

There's a long silence. Bill sits down heavily on a chair; he looks like he's aged about ten years.

"Jeremy is hurt," I say. "Okay? He tried to kill himself, and now he's really badly hurt. Can you please not try to make this all about me?"

Vicky blows out a long sigh. "I'm sorry, Mel. Of course we're worried about Jeremy. But you're always going to be our first concern. We love you."

"I know you do," I say, and it comes out sounding almost rude. "But dragging up something that happened last year isn't exactly helpful, okay?"

"The police said that Melody tried to stop him from jumping," Christine says.

Bill stands up, walks over, wraps his arms around both me and Vicky. "Can she see Jeremy?" he asks. "Or not yet?"

"Probably not yet," Christine says. "He's just come out of surgery."

"I don't want to see him," I say. "I want to go home."

Black Holes

A few weeks ago, at Halloween, Jeremy finally told me what had happened with his brother.

I was taking Suzy trick-or-treating and I'd talked him into coming with us. "It's the perfect excuse to go," I'd told him. "I'm officially babysitting, which means I'm actually getting cash to dress up as a cat and walk around the neighborhood. My first paid acting gig."

He laughed, and after dinner he showed up at my place wearing a long white lab coat, dark-framed glasses and a frizzy gray wig. He looked ridiculous.

"What are you supposed to be?" I asked him.

"Scientist from Transexual Transylvania. *Rocky Horror Show*, you know? But you can tell Suzy I'm Einstein."

I lifted the lapel of his lab coat and peeked underneath. Black T-shirt. "Shouldn't you be wearing sexy lingerie?"

"Yeah, but I didn't want to freak you out too much.

Anyway, I thought I should keep it G-rated for the kid's sake."

"She'll be here any minute." I turned back to the hallway mirror and started drawing whiskers on my cheeks with black eyeliner. "Her mom's dropping her off."

"This is the same kid who did your nails, right?"

"Good memory." I glanced down at what was left of my lime-green shimmer. "She's in third grade. Not your typical third-grader though."

"In what way?"

"Freakishly smart."

"Like you."

"Not like me. I get by okay, but Suzy's in a different league altogether." I met Suzy a year ago, after her mom contacted the coordinator of the early college prep program at my high school, looking for someone who could be a sort of mentor-babysitter-big sister type person for her brainiac kid. I'd rolled my eyes a bit when Mrs. Williams had asked me if I was interested, but she'd offered a decent wage so I'd said yes. I wasn't sure why Mrs. Williams had picked me, out of all the kids in our program, but I was glad she had. Suzy was cool.

The doorbell rang. "Come on," I said. "That'll be her."

"You sure she won't mind me coming too?"

"Yup." I took the stairs two at a time and opened the front door. "Suzy?"

"Hello." Suzy tilted her head, studying me critically.

Her mom, Nina, stood behind her, black hair pulled back in a tight ponytail, gold stud shining in her nose. "Hi, Melody. Thank you for doing this."

"Don't you have cat ears?" Suzy asked abruptly.

"I just haven't put them on yet. See?" I held up a headband with pointed black ears attached to it. "You look awesome, by the way." Suzy was covered head to toe in green feathers. Her hair was gelled up in a wild mess of spikes. In her hand was a silver flute, and a small birdcage dangled from a sash over her shoulder.

"Are you a parrot?" Jeremy asked.

"Papageno."

Jeremy looked at me, eyebrows raised.

"The bird catcher. From *The Magic Flute*," Suzy explained.

He shook his head. "Sorry. Is that a movie?"

"Opera," Nina said. "Mozart."

"Ah." He held out a hand to shake. "I'm Mel's friend Jeremy."

"Nice to meet you." Nina shook his hand and then turned to me. "Have fun, Mel. I'll pick Suzy up at nine, if that's okay? Jim and I are going out for dinner together. At a nice, quiet, adult-oriented restaurant. No crayons, no kids' menus."

I laughed. "Nine's good. Have fun." I waved goodbye,

and she headed back to her car. Jim gave me a grin and a thumbs-up from the driver's seat.

"Hi, Suzy," Jeremy said. "I'm Jeremy. Mel said it would be okay if I joined you guys tonight."

"I know. I told her she could say that."

"So." I slipped my headband on and adjusted the pointy black ears. "It's getting dark. And I can see some kids down the street. Shall we get going?"

"What about your house? Who's going to hand out candy?"

"Vicky's here," I said. "And Bill."

"I want to show them my costume," Suzy said.

"Yeah, come on." I led the way to the living room, where Bill made Suzy's day by doing a very bad rendition of the duet between Papageno and Papagena—*Pa-Pa-Pa-Pa-Pa-Pa-Papagena!* —while Vicky exclaimed over the brilliance of her costume.

We finally made it out the door, and Suzy ran ahead of us down the sidewalk, flapping her arms wildly. "She's a strange one, isn't she?" Jeremy said.

"She's flying."

"I know. But I can see…I mean, she's great, but she's not going to fit in very easily, is she?"

I shook my head and watched Suzy start up my neighbor's driveway. "No. School's hellish for her. Kids are so mean, you know?"

"Yeah." Jeremy cleared his throat. "I do know, actually."

I turned away from Suzy and looked up at him.

Suzy hurtled back toward us. "Tootsie Roll *and* a Snickers! Can I go to the next house?"

"Yeah, of course." We followed her as she flapped her way onward.

Jeremy gestured after Suzy. "I was a weird kid too, I guess. I didn't talk until I was nearly three, and then I just began speaking in full sentences. When I started school, the teacher wanted my parents to get me assessed. They thought I was autistic or something. Mom says I liked to spin in circles. I made funny noises. Stuff like that."

"Kids all do weird stuff." I thought of an old line Bill liked to quote: *All the world is queer, save thee and me, and even thee is a little queer.*

"I guess. I always got teased though. Then Lucas came along, and he was the poster child for normal."

"Mmm." I watched Suzy dash past a group of gauzy princesses tottering in high heels and race up the steps of the next house. "Well, you don't spin in circles anymore."

"No." He cleared his throat again. "I guess I outgrew it or something. Anyway. About what happened to Lucas." Jeremy stared straight ahead, watching the kids clustering around the front door. "It was summer, so just over two years ago. He wanted to go down to the beach with a couple of his friends. Mom made me go with them—she was always trying to get me to do stuff with Lucas; she didn't ever seem to get that he didn't want me there."

"You were supposed to…I mean, she wanted you to—" I bit off the words.

"Keep an eye on him? Yeah." Jeremy's voice was hard.

"Jeremy, whatever happened, it wasn't your fault." I knew as soon as the words were out of my mouth that I'd made a mistake.

"You don't even know what happened, Melody. So don't give me that bullshit line, okay?"

"Sorry. I'm sorry."

"Forget it." He waved at Suzy, who was walking back toward us, treat bag held wide open, lips moving as she counted candies. "How's it going, kiddo? Lots of loot?"

Suzy frowned. I suspected she didn't like the *kiddo*. "Lots of those gross caramels. You want some? I mostly just like chocolate."

Jeremy held out a hand and accepted a caramel. "Thanks, kiddo. I call lots of people kiddo, by the way. Not just kids."

She cracked a hint of a smile. "No problem."

"Babe too. I call Melody babe sometimes." He nudged me. "Don't I, babe?"

"You better not," I told him.

Suzy giggled. "I'm going to that house there, see?

They've got a monster by the porch that moves when you get close. I think it has a motion sensor of some kind."

"Cool."

She scampered off.

"Jeremy," I said. "Look, I didn't mean to upset you. I just...I was worried you were blaming yourself. Just because you were there when Lucas died. But you're right. I don't know what happened."

He nodded. "I shouldn't have snapped at you."

"It's okay."

"I had a dream about him last night," he said.

"Like what you were telling me about? That lucid-dream thing?"

"Yeah. Sort of. I knew I was dreaming, but I couldn't control it. I wanted to talk to him about what happened. To say sorry, I guess."

"Did you?"

"No. He was being such a little snot."

I laughed. "In your dream?"

"Yeah." He gave a reluctant laugh. "I guess that is kind of funny. But he could be so obnoxious, Mel. No one really saw that side of him except me."

"I guess siblings aren't always friends," I said. "I used to have this fantasy about having a brother or sister, but I guess the reality is that you're just stuck with someone and you might not even get along."

Jeremy nodded. "It's hard to say it now, but sometimes I didn't even like him. He was younger, but in some ways, it didn't seem like it."

"How d'you mean?"

"That day at the beach. There was Lucas and two of his friends, Daimon and Carter, and the three of them were basically entertaining themselves by making fun of me. Like they were so cool, and I was…well, not. It was the same crap I got at school, and I'd had enough, you know? I told Lucas to shove it. Went for a walk. When I came back, Daimon and Carter were on the beach playing volleyball with a bunch of other kids, and I couldn't see Lucas. I wasn't really worried. Figured he'd gone to get a burger or maybe was farther down the beach, trying to pick up some girl. Something like that."

"There're lifeguards, right?"

He nodded. "That's who spotted him. But it was too late by then. He was already dead."

"But why did he…I mean, he could swim, right?"

"Yeah, of course. He was a good swimmer." He looked down at the caramel in his hand as if he didn't know how it got there, shoved it into his pocket and stared down the street at all the princesses and vampires and ghosts and Harry Potters and the clusters of parents standing at the ends of the driveways. "He had epilepsy, Mel. Mostly really well controlled by meds."

"He had a seizure? In the water?"

Jeremy nodded. "That's what we think happened. It was the only thing that made sense."

I didn't say anything, but what I was thinking was, So that's why your mom wanted you to go. You were supposed to be watching him.

Which meant it kind of was Jeremy's fault after all. I felt a sharp pain in my chest, like my heart was cracking wide open. Poor Jeremy. How do you live with that? I couldn't imagine it.

No wonder he hadn't wanted to talk about it.

I was trying to think of something to say when Suzy rejoined us. "Look at this," she said. "Candy called Toxic Waste. Is that supposed to be a joke?"

"Uh-huh." I took it from her and looked at the ingredients list. "Though it's probably not too far off. Sugar, yeah, but listen to this: glycerine, artificial flavors, confectionary glaze (shellac, coconut oil, ethanol), artificial colors, blah, blah, blah." I made a face. "That's disgusting."

Jeremy took the candy from me. "Seriously? It says shellac? Isn't that nail polish or something?"

Suzy shook her head. "It's actually a resin secreted by lac bugs."

"Lac bugs," he repeated. "You're kidding me, right?"

"Nope. They live in India. On trees. It's just the females who make the resin."

"Right." Jeremy looked at her with a new respect. "You should go on one of those trivia shows. You'd probably win a million bucks."

Suzy didn't respond. She was on a roll, and when she gets like that there's no stopping her. "It's used in all kinds of things. I read about it on Wikipedia."

"Hope you're not planning to eat it," I said.

"It's edible. They use it to make apples shiny." She shook her head as Jeremy tried to hand the candy back to her. "I don't want it. It's weird to give kids candy packaged as toxic waste. Maybe the people in that house don't like kids."

Jeremy unwrapped it and popped it into his mouth. "Holy sour." He made a bug-eyed face at Suzy and then looked back at me. "I should cut out, Mel. Get home."

"It's early," I said, surprised. "We're not done trick-or-treating."

He shrugged. "Stuff to do. I usually help my mom hand out candy and all that."

"Okay." I wondered if he was feeling uncomfortable, having told me what had happened to Lucas. Then I wondered if Halloween made his mom sad, thinking about all the years her two boys had gone out together. The Blues Brothers, I thought. Salt and pepper shakers. I cleared my throat. "I'll see you at school tomorrow, I guess."

He nodded. "Good to meet you, Suzy."

"Uh-huh." She waved a feathered hand at him and, without waiting for him to actually leave, started talking to me. "Guess what I read today, Mel?"

I mouthed another *bye* to Jeremy. "What?"

"It's about black holes."

I sighed. Suzy's favorite subject was astronomy. I'd already heard more about supernovas and gamma rays and quasars than I ever wanted to know.

"No, this is really cool. You know how stars burn hydrogen, right?"

"Yeah." Only because she'd told me a hundred times.

"Okay. Well, you get a really, really big star—like, one that makes our sun look tiny—and its core is all hydrogen and it's burning up, exploding outward with a lot of force. But because the star is so huge, it also has a ton of gravity, right? Pushing inward."

"They cancel each other out? The two forces?"

"Yeah, basically. Balance each other."

"Cool."

"I'm not even at the cool part yet, Mel." She frowned at me. "Listen. All that hydrogen eventually gets burned up. Used up. Right? And when it's gone, there's just the one force, gravity, pushing in. So the core of the star collapses."

"Weird. Just the core?"

"*First* the core." Suzy bounced up and down on her toes, and the streetlight's pale glow caught on her feathers in a shimmer of color. She looked like the northern lights. "But that core is so dense…it's a baby black hole, Mel. A brand-new baby black hole."

"Cute." I knew this would bug her.

Sure enough, she frowned at me. "Not so cute. Because that baby black hole starts sucking in the star around it. Consuming it. *Cannibalizing* it."

I made a face. "Nice image. Remind me never to have a kid."

"Here's the part that I love. Love love love." She bounced harder than ever and then paused to make sure she had my full attention. "At that point, the star doesn't even know its core has collapsed. From the outside, everything still looks normal."

I gave a sudden involuntary shudder. "That's horrible," I said, more vehemently than I meant to.

Suzy looked taken aback. "It is?"

"Just the idea that, you know, it's dying and it doesn't know it."

"Well, it's just a star. It's not really alive or conscious or anything."

"Yeah, I know." I pointed at her collection of candy. "So. More trick-or-treating, or are you done?"

She jiggled the bag, weighing the loot. "Maybe a few more houses."

I grinned at her. "Onward ho."

Suzy gave a Papageno-style chirp—*Pa-Pa-Pa!*—and dashed off, flapping wildly. I laughed, but I felt chilled deep down inside. I couldn't stop thinking about Jeremy, heading home to hand out candy with his mom, with the stark absence of Lucas between them.

And I couldn't get that image of Suzy's damn star out of my mind.

Lucid Dreams

It must have been a few days after Halloween that Jeremy brought up lucid dreaming again. I remember it clearly, not because it was all that significant in itself, but because it was the closest we'd come to having a fight.

We were at school, sitting by our big oak tree. Jeremy was leaning back against the trunk, wearing faded jeans and a gray, long-sleeved T-shirt that made him look paler and thinner than ever. I was looking at him, trying to figure out if I was attracted to him or not. Everyone assumed that we were a couple, and I thought about him all the time. I wanted to lean up against him, rest my head on his shoulder, stroke his hair. He wasn't exactly good-looking—too skinny, and that beaky nose—but there was something about him that pulled on me.

"I'm quitting smoking," I told him.

"Yeah?"

"After this pack." I couldn't stand how guilty I felt every time I had a cigarette. I kept imagining how upset Vicky and Bill would be. Plus I was so paranoid about them smelling it on me that I sprayed on perfume and brushed my teeth for, like, five minutes before I left school every day.

"Yeah, so you keep saying." Jeremy frowned at me. "Hand it over."

I passed the pack to him, and he opened it. "I'll have this. You're done."

"You hate smoking," I said.

He shrugged. "Maybe I want to learn to blow smoke rings."

"Don't. If you start, I'll feel guilty."

Jeremy rolled his eyes. "Fine. I'll give it to my mom."

"Your mom smokes?" I raised my eyebrows. "And she rolls her own?"

"Yup."

"Fine. She can have it." I looked at him. "So when am I going to meet your parents?"

"My dad, probably never. He moved out a year ago."

"That sucks."

"Yeah. My mom though? You can meet her anytime. You want to?"

I shrugged. "Sure."

"She's out a lot," Jeremy said. "She coaches the girls' track team."

"I thought she was a math teacher."

"Yeah. She is. But she's a runner too. She runs five miles every morning before work."

"And she smokes?" I raised my eyebrows again.

"I lied about the smoking," Jeremy said. "Oops."

I stared at him. It kind of freaked me out that he'd lied so easily. "But she's really a teacher? And a runner?"

"Sure, Mel. Don't panic."

"I'm not *panicking*," I said. "But I don't like being lied to."

"Sorry. Really, Mel. I just wanted to help you quit smoking."

There was an awkward silence, and I felt like we were teetering right on the brink of a fight. I shook my head. "It's okay," I said. "Forget it."

Jeremy grinned at me. "Forgotten. Hey, I meant to tell you: I totally had a lucid dream last night."

I wondered if he'd been able to talk to Lucas this time. "What was it about?"

"Swimming. I was in a pool, swimming along under-water, and I realized I was dreaming. I told myself to stay calm, not wake myself up. I swam to the edge and got out and looked around. There was no one else there at all."

Not even a lifeguard. "So what did you do?" I asked.

"I decided to check the change room. I told myself, Lucas will be in there. He'll be sitting on the bench, putting his shoes on, ready to go. We'll walk out together."

"Did it work?"

"Sort of. He was there, just like I told him to be." Jeremy hesitated. "But when he saw me, he stood up and walked away. He just left. And I ran after him. I followed him out of the change room into the lobby, but he just disappeared. And then I woke up."

"Well, that's progress, right?" I didn't understand why he was so focused on this dream thing. It wasn't like dreaming about his brother was going to bring him back.

"In a way. I mean, I'm getting better at knowing I'm dreaming. But—well, he's refusing to talk to me. He's angry."

I stared at him. "It's a dream, Jeremy. It just means that you're scared he's angry. He's not really angry."

"You don't know that."

"Uh, yeah, I do. He's dead. Dead people aren't angry." I reached out and touched his sleeve. "It was only a dream."

He pulled his arm away. "Some people think dreams are very significant. That they mean more than we think."

"Sure. I mean, I know people interpret dreams and all that," I said, "but I don't see how they can tell you anything about your brother beyond what's already in your head."

"That's because you're just buying into the main-stream way of thinking," Jeremy said. "Some cultures think dreams are powerful. That in dreams, we can actually move from this world into another world."

"Yeah, but—well, you don't really believe that, do you? Anyway, doesn't science kind of take the mystery out of dreaming? I mean, you can hook someone up and see their brainwaves and all that. REM sleep, right? Twitchy eyes?"

He snorted. "Science is a long way from being able to explain dreaming."

"Isn't it something about memory? Transferring stuff from short-term memory to long-term memory? Or something like that. I read an article about it." I made a face. "Geek alert, I know. But my parents keep stacks of old *Scientific American*s in the bathroom."

"There are tons of theories," Jeremy said dismissively. "And they all contradict each other. And none of them really explain why or how we dream."

"And you have the answers, do you?" It came out sounding ruder than I meant it to, and I softened my voice. "It sounds like you have a theory."

He shook his head. "It just seems to me that we have to look beyond science. That maybe the answers are to be found somewhere else, you know? In the spiritual realm. The mystical realm. Some people believe that when you dream, your spirit leaves your body."

"Yeah, and some people believe the earth is flat," I said.

He shook his head. "You know what, Melody? You're being narrow-minded."

"I'm not. I'm just being skeptical." Skepticism is a core value in my family. I felt uncomfortable imagining my parents' reactions to what Jeremy was saying.

"You're being Eurocentric. You're stuck in the dominant Western scientific paradigm and you're not thinking critically. In fact, you're rejecting anything that threatens your way of thinking."

That stung. "That's not fair," I protested. "I'm listening, aren't I?"

He nodded. "Sorry. I just really want you to understand this. Because it's, well, it's really important to me." His cheeks were flushed, eyes shining. "Mel?"

"Okay. I'll read some stuff. Send me some links or whatever, okay?" If he really believed that Lucas was still out there somewhere—and that he could communicate with him through his dreams—I wasn't sure I wanted to hear it.

≈

I babysat Suzy that evening. She lives in Driftwood, which is this incredibly cool little neighborhood on the Big Bayou. You drive under this wrought-iron sign arched over the road, and it's like you enter another world: narrow, winding roads, huge oak trees dripping with moss, thick green ferns and bamboo, and all kinds of wildlife. Sometimes I persuade Suzy to go exploring along the beach, and we've seen everything from squirrels to herons to black racer snakes. Mostly, though, she prefers to be indoors on the computer or reading a book.

Their house is gorgeous—built-in bookshelves, huge windows, even a fireplace. A safe haven. I could kind of see why Suzy didn't want to leave it too often.

That night, I was glad to be there: I wanted a safe haven. Something about my conversation with Jeremy had gotten under my skin. It wasn't just that he was mad at me. I didn't like that—I hate conflict and generally avoid it if I can—but what really bothered me was feeling like his worldview and mine were sort of slipping apart. I just couldn't understand how he could believe things that were so illogical.

As soon as Suzy went to bed, I looked up lucid dreaming on her laptop. The stuff I read seemed straightforward enough. Weird, but there wasn't anything mystical about it. It was just being conscious that you were dreaming, that was all. After a few science-oriented articles, I stumbled upon a link about astral projection, which sounded more like what Jeremy was talking about—stories of people claiming to actually leave their bodies and travel in some other realm. I didn't see how Jeremy could really believe that was possible but wondered if it was his way of coping with what had happened to Lucas. Maybe he needed to believe it. Maybe it wasn't any stranger than any other set of beliefs—heaven, hell, purgatory, reincarnation, whatever.

I heard Suzy shout something, and I leaped to my feet, startled. I opened the door to her room. "Suzy?"

She was fast asleep, her arms flung wide, face flushed and hot. She slept with the light on and the blankets pulled right up to her chin. I pulled her covers back a little and brushed her hair off her forehead. Suzy's ceiling was covered with glow-in-the-dark stars, which she never got to see because she was scared to be alone in the dark. Funny, for a kid so obsessed with astronomy. I'd asked her once what she was afraid of, but she'd just shrugged and said she didn't know. I got up to leave and something caught my eye. A shimmer of green on the floor. I bent down and picked it up: a feather from her Halloween costume.

"Mel?" Suzy opened her eyes and looked at me.

"It's okay," I said. "Just thought I heard you say something, but you must have been talking in your sleep."

She sat up. "I guess I was dreaming."

I perched on the end of her bed. "Bad dream?"

"Not really." A frown creased her forehead. "Just about school. Only there was a beach where the gym should be. It was weird."

"Dreams are weird," I agreed.

"Mel?"

"Mmm."

"What you and Jeremy were talking about on Halloween? About his brother?"

I looked at her, startled. "You overheard that?"

"Just a bit of it. His brother died, right?"

"Yes."

She lay back down and pulled her covers up, tucking them under her chin. "Was he sick?"

"No. He drowned." I bit my lip, wondering about the beach in her dream and whether she had already known that. "I'm sorry you heard that, Suzy. I didn't mean for you to."

"It's okay. I like to know things."

"I know you do."

"Is Jeremy really sad? Is he okay?"

I wasn't sure how okay he was. "He's fine. Don't worry." I stood up. "Go back to sleep, Suzy."

≈

Things were tense at home after Halloween. Vicky was working overtime, trying to drum up public support for her cause, because there was an execution scheduled for November 12. The prisoner's name was Ramon

Hernandez, and he was thirty-six years old. He'd been on death row since he was twenty-two. I knew all about him, because Vicky's friend Pam had made a web page for him. I knew that he was almost illiterate, that he liked listening to audio books, that he enjoyed sketching. I knew why he'd been sentenced to death.

Ramon had stabbed two men in a brawl outside a bar. He hadn't even met them before that night. He'd pulled a knife and two men had died. Vicky said he'd been so drunk he didn't even remember why he was fighting, but he'd stabbed one of them in the throat and the other in the chest, multiple times. It was pretty gruesome to read about. His girlfriend had been there and seen it all happen. She'd testified in court. She was pregnant, but neither of them knew it then.

Around Halloween, Ramon had met his daughter for the first time. Pam hadn't used her name on the website, to protect her privacy, but I knew she lived with her mother and her stepfather in Miami and was the same age as me. I guess her mom thought she should meet her father before he died.

I couldn't imagine it. It bothered me a lot, thinking about her. Knowing that this man who was her father was about to be killed.

Vicky said there wasn't anything we could do to stop it—Ramon's last appeal had been rejected—but she wanted to use the execution to sway some people's opinions about the death penalty. She wanted to give Ramon a human face, to counter the media's attempts to portray him as a monster who was getting what he deserved.

"How come it bothers you so much?" Jeremy asked me.

We were up in my room and I'd just shown him the web page Pam had made for Ramon. His sketches were there, including one he'd done of his daughter. I didn't think anyone was likely to recognize her from it; he wasn't all that skilled an artist. "I don't know," I said. "I think it's because of how deliberate it is. And, you know, official." I shrugged. "It's murder, isn't it? It just feels so wrong."

"Maybe he'll be better off."

"Dead?"

Jeremy shrugged. "I think he'll be back. He'll have another chance. Get this shitty life over with and start fresh."

I looked at him. "Even if you're right and reincarnation is, well, real, it doesn't justify killing him."

He moved away from the computer and flopped down on my couch. "I'd kill myself if I was him. Why wait around?" He picked at his thumbnail. "Sometimes I think I'd rather start over."

His eyebrows were pulled together, lower lip caught between his teeth. His thumb was bleeding where he'd been picking at it. "Jeremy? Are you…okay?"

"No. Not really." He scowled. "I wrote something last night. A poem. You want to see it?"

"Sure."

Jeremy grabbed his backpack, pulled out a notebook and flipped through it. Then he handed it to me. "There. That pretty much says it all."

I took it from him and started reading. *I hate ninety-nine percent of everything*, it began. *I want to delete myself.* His writing was jagged and sharp, all capital letters. I glanced up at him, but he was slumped forward, elbows on his knees, staring down at the floor. I looked back at the poem.

I hate ninety-nine percent of everything,
I want to delete myself.
Annihilate, obliterate…
There's someone always watching.
The aim of life is death
I want to free myself.

"Wow," I said. "Jeremy? That's pretty intense."

"Intense?" He looked up at me, a lopsided, mocking grin on his face. "Yeah, I guess."

"It's really good though," I said hastily. I felt embarrassed, like I'd seen something I didn't want to see.

He shrugged. "I used to write a lot. That's the first thing I've written in a while though."

"Cool," I said. "You're a good writer."

Like that was the point.

Event Horizon

Finally, my parents drive me home from the hospital. I sit in the backseat, behind my mom. Dad drives. None of us are saying much. I'm going over the last two months in my mind, trying to understand. Meeting Jeremy back in September. Hanging out, getting to know each other. His obsession with lucid dreams and with seeing his brother again. Trick-or-treating—he'd been okay that night, chatting with Suzy. He'd seemed fine. But that poem he wrote…and the things he said the day of the execution…

"Melody?" Bill says softly. "Please don't blame yourself for this. When someone commits suicide—or, well, attempts it—it's normal to think about what you could have done. How you could have prevented it. But please don't. There's no way you could have seen this coming."

He's wrong, of course, but he has no way of knowing just how far down this path I walked with Jeremy. And I don't know where or when we crossed the line. I don't know when we slipped from kidding around to planning to die together. And that makes me think of something else Suzy told me about. The event horizon.

I lean against the window and close my eyes, and I picture Suzy's dark eyes fixed on me as she's pacing back and forth, bouncing on her toes as she talks. "The event horizon—it's like the edge of a black hole, but it isn't a physical thing. Once you've crossed it, though, that's it. You're basically doomed to get sucked into the black hole."

"Point of no return, huh?" I'd said, only half listening.

"Exactly," Suzy had said.

I open my eyes and look out the window, watching the streetlights flash by, and I wonder when Jeremy crossed the event horizon. And I wonder how I didn't see it, and how much of the blame belongs squarely on my own shoulders.

I know what my dad is trying to say: it isn't all about me. In the last two years, Jeremy lost his brother and his dad. His mom's still there, but she's not the kind of person I could imagine confiding in.

I'm the only one Jeremy actually talked to. I'm the only one who could have seen this coming.

≈

The first time I met Jeremy's mother was accidental; I don't think Jeremy was in any hurry to introduce us.

It was after Halloween, and we'd stopped by his place after school to pick up new batteries and a memory card for his camera. We were doing some photography together for WaitingToDie.com, Vicky and Pam's death-row website—wandering around town taking semi-random, artsy pictures of chain-link fences and padlocks and anything that might symbolize prison.

Jeremy's place was huge and expensive-looking—a ranch-style house with landscaping that fit right in with the nearby country club. "Wow," I said. "This place is amazing."

"Yeah." Jeremy opened the front door. "We're going to have to sell it though. Mom doesn't want to move, but she can't afford to buy Dad out."

"How long ago did they split up?" I stepped inside and looked around. Pale carpets, leather couches, glass coffee table and none of the warmth and clutter of my house. It was oddly generic, like a show home or a tastefully decorated hotel suite. You couldn't tell anything about the people who lived here.

"A year ago." He slipped his shoes off.

"Have you always lived here?"

"Since I was four." He shrugged. "So as long as I remember."

I scanned the living room for personal touches and my gaze landed on two framed photographs on the piano: a recent school picture of Jeremy, unsmiling, and beside it a photograph of what had to be Lucas. The younger boy was fair-haired, tanned and freckled, grinning—the opposite of Jeremy but with similar features, like a photographic negative. I imagined Jeremy's photo changing, being replaced by a new one each year, while Lucas's stayed the same, frozen in time, the gap between them ever increasing.

"That's Lucas?" I asked softly.

He nodded. "That's Lucas. Yeah."

"Jeremy?" A voice called out, and I heard footsteps coming down the stairs.

"Mom?"

A tall woman stepped into the living room. "I came home early. Thought I was getting a migraine, and I didn't have any of my pills at work." She was almost as thin as Jeremy but with more muscle. She looked like a runner, I thought. A marathon runner. Sinewy, not an ounce of fat on her. She had the kind of smoothly styled hair that probably took forty minutes every morning, and under it a smooth mannequin face, slender arched eyebrows, neutral-tone lipstick. Vicky's age, probably—fortyish—but as different from my own mother in appearance as it was possible for two women the same age to be.

"Uh, we're just picking something up," Jeremy said quickly. "Sorry. Mom, this is Melody."

I held out my hand. "Nice to meet you, Mrs. Weathers."

She shook my hand, eyeing me appraisingly. Her nails were long and expertly manicured. I felt my cheeks getting hot as I wondered what she was thinking about finding her son in the house with a girl. Her voice was tense and cool. "Well," she said, "I'm going to go lie down. If you could keep the noise down, I'd appreciate it."

"We're going to Melody's house," Jeremy said.

I followed Jeremy to his room and watched him change the batteries and memory card in his camera. I couldn't stop thinking about Lucas the whole time we were there— it was as if the sadness had saturated the carpets and drapes, soaked into the upholstery, permeated the very foundation of the house. I wondered what they had done about Lucas's bedroom and what it meant to Jeremy to be leaving this house. If I was him, I'd be glad to leave. It was the kind of house that made you feel hyperconscious of being a visitor.

"Jeremy?" I said, once we were back outside in the fresh air and sunshine. "Do you ever feel sort of like a guest in there?"

"In my house?" He looked at me like I was nuts. "No. Why would I?"

"Just, you know, how tidy it is. And quiet."

He shrugged. "My mom's a neat freak. Anyway, you saw my room."

Jeremy's room might have been messy by his mom's standards, but it didn't look like any teenager's room I'd ever seen before. Three or four books piled on his bedside table—all nonfiction, I'd noticed—and a sweatshirt tossed carelessly on the floor. That was about as far as rebellion seemed to go in his house. "Your room's not messy," I said. "Not even close."

"Yeah. I guess. Mom's kind of OCD, actually," Jeremy said. "She couldn't take it if my room looked like yours. Not that there's anything wrong with your room. But she needs everything to be put away in its place, you know?"

"Mmm." I ran my fingers along a fence as we walked, feeling the rhythmic bump-bump-bump of the wooden boards.

Jeremy stopped walking and took a picture of the fence. "She's had some problems," he said. "Depression, that sort of thing." He cleared his throat. "I don't like to add to her stress. That's all. It's no big deal to keep things tidy."

"I guess she's had a lot to deal with," I said. "Lucas dying, and then, you know. What happened with your dad."

"Nothing *happened*." Jeremy turned and looked at me, his eyes wary and his voice hard. "They split up. That's all."

"Yeah. I know. That's what I meant." I felt like I'd offended him somehow. "Did I say something I shouldn't have?"

He shook his head. "No. Just don't mention him around my mother, okay?"

"Okay." Not like I was ever around his mother anyway. "Do you see much of him?"

"No. No, he's…he moved out of town."

I dropped the subject after that.

Waking

Vicky wakes me up. Even before I open my eyes, yesterday comes rushing in: the hours at the hospital, Jeremy falling from the bridge. The sun is streaming in my window and I can see the deep etching of crow's-feet around my mother's eyes as she bends over me.

"Jeremy's mom is on the phone, Mel. I thought you might want to take it." She holds a phone out toward me and sees my hesitation. "It's okay. Good news."

I clear my throat and take the phone from her. "Mrs. Weathers?"

"Hi, Melody. I just wanted to let you know Jeremy's conscious and doing well. They're saying he'll be fine." She sounds like she did the first time I met her—controlled, cool, intimidating. Nothing like the frantic woman I saw at the hospital last night.

"Is he awake?" I wonder what he has told her.

"Yes." She gives a little cough. "He wants to see you."

"Oh. He does?"

"Yes."

There is an awkward pause. I want to see Jeremy too. At least, part of me does.

The rest of me—the larger part—is terrified.

"Okay," I say. "I'll be there as soon as I can."

After I hang up the phone, I look at Vicky. "He's awake. He wants to see me. Can you give me a ride?"

She nods. "Of course."

≈

Jeremy is lying in a narrow hospital bed, pale blue sheets pulled up to his chest. He's wearing a hospital gown and he has an IV dripping fluid into the back of his hand. He's even paler than usual, and his eyes are closed, his eyelashes spiky black lines against his cheeks. I sit in a beige plastic chair beside his bed, chip Suzy's latest polish (dark blue and sparkly) off my fingernails and listen to the voices murmuring in the hall outside his room.

"You know how I said we used to fight? Me and Lucas?"

I look at him, startled. I hadn't realized he was awake.

"I liked being an older brother," Jeremy says. "Maybe more than I liked Lucas, you know? It was part of who I was. And then when he died, I wasn't that anymore. Not a big brother."

I don't know what to say, so I just stare at him. His eyes are still closed and his face is eggshell white against the pale blue pillowcase. His voice is slurred, and I figure he's probably doped up on morphine. After a long minute, I clear my throat. "What you said before about reincarnation…do you really believe that? That if you'd died, you guys would be together again somehow?"

"I did," he says. A tear leaks out the corner of his eye and trickles down into his dark hair. "I think I really did."

Past tense. I wonder if he meant to say it that way.

When he opens his eyes, he looks right at me for the first time. "Mel."

"Yeah."

"When I jumped? That exact moment when I jumped, when I started to fall? I realized that I'd just made the biggest fucking mistake of my life."

"You did?" I remember the pale oval of his face looking up at me.

"I didn't want to die," he says. "I didn't *want* to." His face twists, and he sounds incredulous, like this makes no sense to him. "I tried to fall straight, you know? Legs together, feet first, all tucked in close. I didn't want to die."

I swallow. "It must have hurt."

"Mmm. Yeah. It was like hitting cement." He laughs. "Not funny. Sorry. I'm kind of stoned." He lifts one hand slightly, indicating the bag of clear liquid hanging from the IV pole.

"I thought you'd hate me," I whisper. "For not jumping."

"No. Never." He shakes his head, winces, presses a hand to his side. "I'd hate myself if you had. God, if you'd died and I hadn't…I couldn't take one more thing to feel guilty about."

"Jeremy…"

"I didn't even lose consciousness when I hit the water." He looks at me. "I remember thinking I had to try to swim, but everything hurt so bad. I guess I passed out at some point, because I remember being pulled out of the water, sort of, and the next thing is, I'm waking up in this room."

"I'm so glad you're still here," I say. "I thought for sure…"

"I'm glad too, I guess." He licks his lips. "Is there any water?"

"I can get you some," I say, glad to have a purpose. "I'll be right back."

When I step back into his room a minute later, plastic cup of ice water in my hand, Jeremy is asleep. I put the cup on the small table beside his bed and watch his chest slowly rising and falling for over an hour before I head down to find Vicky in the hospital coffee shop.

≈

Apparently the rumor mill is working even on the weekend, because the next day, for the first time in a very long time, my phone is buzzing with texts from Adriana and Devika. OMG heard about J! Call me!

Not likely.

"Maybe you should call them," Vicky says softly. We're sitting on the couch together drinking tea, reading and passing the Sunday paper's crossword puzzle back and forth. "Might make tomorrow easier, if you get this out of the way."

"Tomorrow?" I put the newspaper down.

"At school."

I hadn't even thought about it. "I haven't talked to them in forever."

"I know." She made a face. "It doesn't mean that they aren't genuinely concerned about you though."

I snort. "They want the inside scoop so they can tell everyone. Gossip is social currency."

"You three used to be such good friends. Maybe you should give them another chance, Mel."

I don't bother replying. Another chance to do what? Call me names, spread rumors, make me feel like shit? I don't think so.

≈

Monday morning I can feel the stares and sense the whispers as soon as I walk into the school. I don't know how it happened, but it's obvious that the story, or some warped version of it, is out there. Adriana and Devika sidle up to me at my locker after homeroom.

"Hi, Mel," Adriana says.

I look at her and Devika and raise my eyebrows. I have less than nothing to say to either of them.

Adriana hesitates, chewing on her lower lip for a moment. She's got her braces off, I notice. I remember when she first got them, at the start of grade seven. She cried and cried. "I heard that your boyfriend tried to kill himself," she whispers.

"Jeremy isn't my boyfriend," I say.

"Well, your friend, then." She looks to Devika for help.

"Is he, you know, going to be okay?" Devika says.

"How'd you hear about it?" I ask, wondering if they know I was there.

"My mom knows someone who's in a running group with his mother," Adriana says.

"Right." And I'm sure Jeremy's mom really appreciates her running buddies fueling the rumor mill. "Well, yeah, he's going to be okay."

"What did he do?" Devika asks. "Like, did he take an overdose?"

Adriana's freckled cheeks are pink, and I wonder if she's thinking about that awful party and the Tylenol and how she called the ambulance. "None of your business," I say.

"Sorry. I just wondered." Devika tucks her smooth dark hair behind her ears. "I mean, you don't have to talk about it if you don't want to."

"I know." I shut my locker door and fasten the combination lock. "Excuse me."

Devika shrugs and steps aside, but Adriana hesitates for a second. "Mel. Um. I just wondered, you know, if you were okay."

I scowl at her. "I'm not planning to kill myself, if that's the kind of gossip you're hoping for. No, wait, it doesn't matter what I'm planning, does it? You can spread that rumor anyway. Get the whole Death Wish thing going again."

"I didn't…That wasn't…"

"Whatever," I say, pushing past her.

≈

Ten minutes into math class, I get called down to the office. My mouth is dry and my heart flutters wildly as I hurry down the hallway. I'm not sure what I'm afraid of, but there's this awful nameless dread in my belly.

"Oh, Melody," the receptionist says. "Mrs. Paulsen wants to see you in counseling services."

I've never met Mrs. Paulsen before. Never been to counseling services, which turns out to be just one small office beside the medical room. Posters line the wall outside. I can't tear my eyes away from the hideous before and after photos of crystal meth users.

"Melody? Come on in, please. Sit down." Mrs. Paulsen is an older woman with short, curly gray hair and a white cardigan; her taste in artwork seems to be of the inspirational kitten variety. *Hang in there! Things are looking up!*

I take a seat in a pale blue chair and wait to see where this is going.

"You're probably wondering why you're here," she says.

"I'm assuming it's about Jeremy."

"Yes. A couple of people mentioned that he was a good friend of yours."

"Is."

"Pardon?" She looks confused.

"Is a good friend of mine. Present tense. He's not dead."

Mrs. Paulsen nods. "A very lucky young man, from what I understand."

"Which is what?" I ask, feeling mean but nonetheless taking pleasure in being difficult.

"I spoke with his mother," she says. "She said that you were with him when he jumped from the bridge."

My heart thuds out of rhythm, an almost painful jarring kick in the chest. I have to remind myself that she wasn't there. She doesn't know. "Yes."

"She said you tried to stop him."

My eyes are suddenly swimming. "Not hard enough," I say. It might be the first truthful thing I've said about this.

"Mrs. Weathers was worried about you," she says. "It's very common for people to blame themselves when things like this happen."

"Yeah, I guess."

"Do you want to tell me about it?" She crosses her legs and leans toward me.

"Not really."

"Sometimes it helps to talk."

I don't say anything. I imagine my skin hardening into a shell around me, impermeable, impenetrable.

"I don't want to make you uncomfortable," she says. Her glasses are so clear they look like they don't even have lenses in them. "I just wanted to make sure you knew that you can come and talk to me anytime, if you need support. And Jeremy, of course, when he returns to school."

"Right. Okay."

She leans back and sighs. "I have a book you might like to borrow." She turns, reaches behind her and slides a book off the shelf.

I take it from her. *Surviving the Suicide of a Loved One.* On the front cover, a rose with a falling petal. "Jeremy's not dead," I tell her for the second time.

"I know," she says. "But you should read the chapter on survivor guilt anyway. I don't want you to blame yourself for what he did."

No one does: Mrs. Weathers, Vicky and Bill, the hospital social worker, now Mrs. Paulsen. I'm pretty sure they'd all feel a whole lot different if they knew exactly what had happened.

———

It wasn't any single event that led us to the Skyway Bridge. When I look back, when I try to sift through everything that happened, the memories pile up in a crazy, unstoppable cascade, each one leading to another, bringing us closer and closer to the moment we stood together at the very edge. To the moment Jeremy jumped, and I didn't.

If it wasn't for me, Jeremy would never have been on that bridge. It's not just that I was the first to suggest jumping off the bridge—though that would have been bad enough—or even that I added my own songs to his suicide playlist. What bothers me is that at Halloween I already knew that something was really wrong. And after Halloween, things went steadily downhill. Looking back, I can see screaming red flags scattered throughout the landscape of our conversations, but I'd ignored every warning sign.

No. It was worse than that. I'd embraced it. It was romantic to me, all that darkness. It was what drew us together, and so I did what I could to feed it. I joined Jeremy there without even seeing what a dangerous place he was standing in.

Drowning

A week before Ramon's execution, Jeremy and I skipped out of school. He'd taken his mom's car, not exactly something she'd agreed to.

"Better to ask forgiveness than permission," he said. "Not that I'll have to do either as long as we're back before she gets home from work."

I raised my eyebrows. "Thought you didn't like to add to her stress."

"What she doesn't know won't hurt her," he said shortly.

He sounded angry—bitter, almost—but I let it go by. The sky was blue and I was high about skipping school and heading out on an illicit road trip with Jeremy, and I didn't want to ruin the mood by getting into anything heavy. "Got any tunes?" I asked. "Or are we listening to the radio?"

He handed me his iPhone and I found us some road-trip music. "So where do you want to go?"

"Want to see the prison?" I asked. "There're protesters outside every day now. Mom was there on the weekend, and she said there were a lot of people there with signs and stuff. Because of Ramon, you know?"

"Yeah, you told me." He shrugged. "Jacksonville's a three-hour drive. We'd get there and it'd be time to turn around and come home again."

"I guess," I said. I didn't know why I wanted to go there anyway. It was the same impulse that makes you pick at hangnails until they're bloody and sore—I hated to think about it, but I couldn't leave it alone.

"Let's go to the beach," Jeremy said. "I'll show you where Lucas drowned."

I turned and looked at him. "Seriously? I mean, you sure you want to do that?"

He didn't answer, just started the engine and reversed out of the school parking lot. After a few minutes, the silence between us was making me squirm. "Have you had more dreams about him?" I asked.

Jeremy nodded. "More like nightmares."

I watched his profile, his mouth a hard straight line, his hands tight on the steering wheel. I was almost scared to talk to him when he was like this—so tightly wound, it felt like the wrong word could trigger an explosion. The air between us was electric. "Maybe you shouldn't try so hard, you know?" I said softly. "I mean, trying to dream about him? Maybe it's too—"

"Crazy?"

"No! I didn't mean that. Just, if it's giving you nightmares…"

"I need to talk to him," Jeremy said.

I opened a bag of potato chips, took one and crunched it too loudly. "Want some?"

"No thanks."

We drove in silence for a few minutes, turning onto Pinellas Bayway. The sun shone down on the blue water to our left and right, and pelicans dive-bombed the smooth surface, beautiful and ungainly and vaguely prehistoric.

Finally, Jeremy turned onto Gulf Boulevard and parked at the side of the road. "Well, here we are," he said. Through my window, I stared at the white beach and the blue-gray water, and all I could think was, Lucas swam into that water and never came out again.

≈

We walked along the beach for a while, watching the waves gently lapping the sloping sand. It was pretty quiet: the summer tourists had gone, and the snowbirds were just starting to arrive for the winter. Little kids dug in the sand; their parents lay on beach chairs nearby, reading or chatting. A golden retriever fetched a tennis ball from the water and galloped out, shaking water from its thick coat. A group of shirtless guys played Frisbee. Not locals, obviously: people who live here don't go shirtless in November.

At some point I reached out and took Jeremy's hand in mine, and he didn't pull away.

In front of a small hotel with a blue-and-white awning, Jeremy stopped. "This is the spot," he said abruptly. "We had our towels spread out here. Beach volleyball net was set up over there. Lucas and his friends were swimming. It was July. Stinking hot. I walked off down the beach." He gestured ahead and I stared into the sun, squinting. "And then when I came back, Daimon and Carter were playing volleyball. I figured Lucas was around, you know? I didn't even look for him. Just sat down on my towel and read for a while. Then there was all this commotion. The lifeguard pulled him up on the beach and all these people crowded around—they were doing CPR."

"Oh, Jeremy." I felt stupid and useless and, at the same time, horribly fascinated.

"His face was really white," he said. "Grayish, almost. His lips were blue. They were pounding on his chest so hard, but it didn't work. Water came out of his mouth."

I could feel my eyes filling with tears. I wanted to tell him to stop talking, but maybe it was good that he was sharing this. Vicky would think so, I told myself. She'd say, Let him talk.

"It felt really unreal," Jeremy said. "I kept thinking it'd be okay. That he'd just sit up and crack a joke, you know? And it'd all be okay."

"Yeah," I said. "I guess it must have been hard to believe it could really happen."

Jeremy looked me in the eyes for a second and then looked away. "The ambulance came, and I went with him to the hospital. I called my parents from the beach. When they were still doing CPR."

I wished he was talking to Vicky, not me. To someone who would know the right thing to say, because I sure didn't. "What did you say?" I whispered.

"It was my father who answered the phone. I remember that. And I said there'd been an accident, that Lucas was hurt. They came to the hospital. They didn't know he was already dead. They found out when they got there."

"God, Jeremy. I can't imagine how awful that must have been."

He sat down on the sand and wrapped his arms around his knees. "This is the first time I've been back here."

I knelt beside him and awkwardly put an arm around him. His shoulder blades were sharp ridges under the thin gray T-shirt. "Are you okay?"

"No." His head was on his arms, his face hidden, but I could hear the tears thickening his voice. "Not really."

"I guess not," I said. "I mean, of course not. I'm so sorry, Jeremy." I wanted to tell him that it wasn't his fault, but I thought he'd get angry. And besides, I didn't even know if it was true. In a way, it didn't matter. I watched the waves rolling up onto the sand and thought that I would never look at the ocean the same way again.

After a few minutes, Jeremy lifted his head. "Sorry, Mel. I guess I'm not much fun to be with, huh?"

"No! God, Jeremy. I mean, it's fine. I'm glad you told me about it."

"He hadn't had a seizure in three years," Jeremy said. "I don't want you to think I just…"

"Yeah, no. I don't. Besides, he wasn't alone, right? I mean, he was with his friends when you left him."

Jeremy shrugged. "I doubt they even knew he had epilepsy. He wouldn't have told them. He wouldn't even wear a medic-alert bracelet. Didn't fit his image."

I hesitated. "Your parents…I guess they were still together when that happened?"

"Yeah." His whole body stiffened and he looked away. "My dad left a year later."

"Do you ever see him?"

"No."

I held my breath for a few seconds. "How come, Jeremy?"

"You can probably guess," he said.

He blamed you. I couldn't bring myself to say it though. "No," I said. "I'd have thought…I mean, he'd already lost one of his kids. I would have thought he'd hang on tighter than ever to his other one. You're all he has."

Jeremy snorted. "Right."

I sat beside him, staring out at the water, waiting to see if he wanted to say more. A woman jogged past, pausing occasionally to throw the tennis ball for the golden retriever. An elderly couple walked by, between us and the water. The man had a bent back and took each step slow, leaning on his wife's arm. She was heavier, sturdier-looking, her short white hair ruffled by the breeze.

Finally, I couldn't bear the silence any longer. "What happened? With you and him, I mean?"

"He's an asshole," Jeremy said. "That's what happened."

"To you? Or your mom?"

He shrugged. "Both, I guess."

"Maybe it'd be different now," I said. "You know? I mean, maybe he just couldn't cope with, you know, with Lucas dying. But if you haven't seen him for a year…If you got in touch with him…"

"I think about it sometimes." Jeremy turned and looked at me. "I think he hates me though."

"He can't hate you," I said. "You're his kid."

"Lucas was his favorite, you know? He was everyone's favorite." His Adam's apple jumps as he swallows. "I think my parents felt that the wrong kid died."

"Of course they didn't," I said. "Jeremy, that's awful."

"You didn't know him."

"But I know you." Tears blurred my vision. "Jeremy..." I reached out for him, and he let me pull him into my arms, burying his head against my shoulder.

"This is pathetic," he said, his voice muffled. "Sorry, Mel."

"Jesus, Jeremy. Quit apologizing."

"Some fun day out at the beach, huh?" He lifted his head and looked at me. "You're probably wishing you'd stayed at school. I mean, shit. You could be doing calculus right about now."

"No." I met his eyes. "I'm glad you told me, Jeremy. I'm glad we're here."

"Yeah?"

And right then, something shifted between us. Something in the way he was looking at me, his head tilted to one side. It was ever so slight, but I could feel it. "Yeah," I said. Our faces were inches apart. My heart was racing.

Jeremy reached out a hand and ever so softly touched my cheek. "Don't cry."

"I'm not."

He lifted his wet fingertips to show me. "Are too."

"Well, I'm fine," I said. *Kiss me,* I thought. *Kiss me. Kiss me. Kiss me.*

"Good," he said. He stood up, held out a hand to me. "Come on. Let's blow this popsicle stand."

I took his hand, and as we headed back to the car, I wasn't sure whether the sudden lightness in my chest was disappointment or relief.

Water Under the Bridge

Apparently Jeremy's suicide attempt has turned me into a magnet for the morbidly curious. The story—or at least the bare fact that he jumped from the Sunshine Skyway Bridge—is now public knowledge, and all day I catch people sneaking sideways looks at me and whispering to each other.

After school, Adriana is waiting by my locker. In front of my locker, actually. "Excuse me," I say.

"Mel, please listen to me for a minute." Her reddish blond hair is tied back but a few curls have pulled loose, sticking out in a frizz at her temples.

"You're in my way," I say coldly.

She steps to one side but doesn't leave. I pull a few random books out of my locker and cram them into my backpack, unable to concentrate enough to figure out what I actually need to bring home.

"Mel, I'm sorry, okay? I never meant all that stuff to happen."

"What stuff would that be?" I straighten up so I can watch her squirm. *I don't need you,* I think. *I don't need you. I don't care what you think.*

Her cheeks are flushed, but she stands her ground. "You're not being fair, you know."

"*I'm* not being fair? Hello?" I slam my locker door shut. "Are you fucking serious? You made my life hell."

"I didn't mean to," she says. "I mean, that party…you were freaking out. I didn't know how much Tylenol you'd taken or what else you were going to do. I called 9-1-1 because I was scared, okay? I didn't want you to die." She bursts into tears. "I thought you might understand that now. Because of your friend."

I stare at her and feel like a snow globe someone just picked up and shook—scraps of stuff whirling in my head in a white confusion. What she did—what I have never forgiven her for—is exactly what I failed to do. I didn't call 9-1-1. I didn't save my friend. I didn't take the chance of making him angry, of losing the friendship. "I'm not spreading rumors about Jeremy," I say, trying to hold on to something.

"I didn't mean that to happen," she says. "I mean, after you got taken off in the ambulance, Devika and I had to say something. And it just kind of spun out of control."

"*Death Wish*? Was that part of what you and Devika just had to say?"

"I don't even know who started that," she says. "It wasn't me though. And anyway, it was as much about how you were dressing, you know, all in black. It was like you just became a different person."

I snort. "You and Devika were the ones that changed. As soon as I said I was going to do the early college prep thing, you guys basically dumped me."

"We didn't. You dumped us." She rubs her sleeve across her wet eyes. "It doesn't matter. Water under the bridge."

I wish she hadn't used that expression. Instantly, I'm back there, leaning over that concrete wall, looking down into the inky darkness below.

"Maybe we can just forget about it. Move on," she says.

"Right. Whatever." I sling my backpack over my shoulder. "I gotta go."

"Okay. Just...Mel?"

"What?"

"I'm really sorry, okay? If I did the wrong thing."

I blink back tears and turn away from her, pushing through the crowds in the hallway and out the doors. It's cool and clear, the sky its usual unrelenting blue, and I cross the street and sit down on the steps where I first met Jeremy.

All this time, I've been so angry with Adriana. And now I don't know what to think.

≈

When I get home, Vicky is sitting at the kitchen table with her laptop in front of her.

"Jeremy called," she says.

"He did?" I freeze, heart racing. "What did he say? Did you talk to him?"

"Not much. He's feeling better—well, less drugged anyway. I talked to his mother earlier and she said he's in a lot of pain."

"You talked to his mother? How come?"

"She called."

I'm dying to know what they talked about, but I don't want to ask. She closes her laptop and turns toward me. "He wants to talk to you. I said you'd call when you got home."

"Okay." I start to back away, but she gestures for me to stay.

"How was school?"

"Fine."

"Melody."

"What?"

"Sit down and talk to me."

I sit, reluctantly. "About what?"

"Honey. Don't shut me out, okay? I'm worried about you."

"Well, don't be. I'm not the one who jumped off a bridge."

Vicky flinches, fine lines creasing the skin between her eyes. "You sound angry."

I am angry, but I don't know why, and I don't want to talk about it. "There's nothing to say, Vicky. I mean, of course I'm upset. Wouldn't you be?"

"Of course I would. I *am*. I feel bad that I didn't realize your friend was so depressed."

I hadn't thought of Jeremy as depressed, although, remembering that poem he wrote, maybe I should have. But everyone talks like that sometimes, and he'd been laughing and kidding around with me right up until that night. Right up until he jumped, practically. "Me too," I say. "But there's nothing I can do about it now."

She sighs. "Well, I don't want to push you. But if you want to talk…"

"Okay." I lick my lips, which are suddenly dry. "Um, I guess I'll go call him."

"Good." She opens her laptop. "Oh, and call Nina too. She wants to know if you can babysit Suzy tonight."

"Can I?"

"If you want, sure. I can drive you over there. But maybe you should talk to Jeremy first? I think he was hoping you'd come and see him."

≈

Up in my room, I flop on my couch and call Nina. I'm sort of hoping she needs me right away, so that there isn't time to visit Jeremy, but it turns out she doesn't need me until eight.

"Just for an hour or two, Mel. Jim's away for a few days and I want to go out for tea with a friend whose jerk of a husband walked out on her. Ten years together and he just told her he was moving out. She had no idea. Completely shell shocked. At least they don't have kids."

"That's fine," I say. "I'll be there by eight."

"Need us to pick you up?"

"No, Vicky says she can drive me. Tell Suzy I'm looking forward to seeing her."

I disconnect and call Jeremy.

"Hi, Mel."

He sounds so normal. "Hey," I say. "How are you feeling?"

"Like I got hit by a truck," he says. "Like I jumped off a bridge."

Are we seriously going to joke about this? "Yeah," I say. "I guess you're pretty banged up."

"A couple broken ribs and a cracked vertebra. Doctors say I'll be back on my feet in a few days. Oh, and I'm officially down one internal organ. Luckily, it turns out spleens aren't essential. One of those spare parts you don't really need, like appendixes and tonsils. Who knew?"

"You looked pretty awful," I say.

"Yeah, Mom told me you came to see me already," he says. "I don't even remember it."

"You were pretty out of it."

"Did I say anything weird?"

"You talked about your brother," I say.

There's a silence on the other end of the line, and then Jeremy says, "Can you come and see me? Like, now?"

"Yeah." I stand up. "I'll see you soon."

<hr />

Vicky drives me to the hospital and, to my relief, doesn't try to start another conversation about how I am feeling. She's always been pretty careful about respecting my privacy, but I know she's worried. I wish I knew what Jeremy's mother said to her. I guess this is an awful thing to think, but I'm kind of glad Jeremy and his mom don't have a close relationship. Hopefully, he hasn't told her that I was the one who first suggested jumping off the bridge.

Vicky and I walk up to Jeremy's ward together. "I'll just pop my head in and say hi," she tells me. "Then I'll leave so you two can talk."

"Okay." The hallway smells like antiseptic. My hands are sweaty and my heart is fluttering like it did the time Jeremy and I sat in his kitchen and each drank six cappuccinos in a row. It was one of the very few times we hung out at his house. His mother had this coffee maker that frothed the milk and everything.

"Mel?"

"What?"

"You look tense." Vicky stops walking, puts her hand under my chin and lifts my face toward her. "Are you all right?"

I blink back tears. "Just, you know. This is weird."

She pulls me in for a hug, and I feel like a little kid.

≈

Jeremy is awake, propped up on his pillows into a half-sitting position. He doesn't have the IV bag hooked to his arm anymore, and he's wearing a gray hoodie over his hospital gown. His eyes are clear and focused, and he smiles when he sees us. "Hey, Mel. Vicky! Hi."

"Hi," I say.

Vicky crosses the room. "I'm going to give you a very, very careful hug," she says and puts one arm around him lightly. "There. How are you feeling, Jeremy?"

I'm glad she's here, breaking the ice. Otherwise I might just stand here like an idiot, not knowing what to say.

"Um, embarrassed, mostly," he says. "Otherwise, not too bad, as long as I don't cough or sneeze or laugh. Or move. Or, you know, breathe."

Vicky smiles. "Good. Well, I'm going to head down and get a coffee. Let you two talk. Mel?"

"What?"

"Don't make him laugh."

I can't imagine it, but I force a smile and wave bye as she leaves.

"Here, come sit down," Jeremy says.

I sit down in the beige chair and pull it closer, wincing as it makes a screeching noise on the tile floor. "So. Um, you look better than you did yesterday."

"Yeah. I'm pretty sore, but it sounds like I'm going to be sticking around after all." He shakes his head. "All kind of hard to take in, you know?"

I nod, unable to speak.

"Hey, are you crying? What is it, Mel? I'm okay. Don't." He reaches a hand toward me, and I take it in both of mine. "Talk to me."

"I just…" I try to hold back the tears, but my voice wobbles all over the place. "I thought you were dead, Jeremy. I couldn't believe you did it."

"I know. I'm sorry, Mel." He looks right at me, his eyes serious. "I didn't think about how it would affect you."

Because I was supposed to jump with you. I rub my fingertips lightly against the back of his hand. "I still can't believe it. That you jumped."

"I wasn't sure I was going to. Not right up to the last minute."

"I should've stopped you," I say.

He shakes his head.

I'm scared to ask, but I have to know. "Could I have talked you out of it? I mean, if I'd begged you not to do it, would you have listened?"

"I don't know. Maybe." He shrugs. "Maybe I wouldn't have done it, like, right then. But I'd probably have done it the next day or the next week."

I pull one hand away from Jeremy's to wipe my eyes. "But I didn't even try to stop you. I mean, that's what everyone thinks. That I was up there with you because I was trying to stop you. That's what I told them. Because, you know, I couldn't tell them…"

"I know. It's cool, Mel. Quit beating yourself up."

"But it was my idea, Jeremy. I mean, the bridge thing. I was the one who actually suggested it."

"Were you? I don't remember how that started. It wasn't like I hadn't thought about it before." He squeezes my hand. "If it helps, I think this was something I had to do."

"That's crazy. No one has to jump off a bridge."

"No, I'm serious. I think I needed to do that. I mean, I feel better now than I've felt in a long time. Happier."

And he looks it, too. He's got this smile on his face...It's not like I haven't seen him smile before, but this isn't his usual mocking grin. It's weirdly peaceful and un-Jeremy-like in its sincerity. "So jumping off the bridge made you happy? That makes no sense at all."

"I think I had to face death, you know?"

"No, I don't know." I stare at him. "Jeremy, it was a total fluke that you survived."

"I don't think so," he says. "I don't believe that."

"Of course it was! You know the stats on that bridge." My voice is rising, and I have to force myself to take a breath and talk softly. "There must be dozens of deaths for every survivor."

"Exactly," Jeremy says. His voice is triumphant, like he's just proved a point. "The odds were against me surviving, but I did."

"But you could just as easily have died. So to say you had to do it makes no sense at all." I feel like I am talking to a wall, like he's not really hearing me.

"I just think I survived for a reason," he says.

I remember what he said before, about trying to fall straight. "You mean because you realized you'd made a mistake? Because you decided you wanted to live?"

"More than that," he says. "I don't know. But Mel, when I was in the water and everything hurt and I saw that boat coming for me…the lights on the water…I was in absolute agony, but somehow I knew everything was going to be okay. Better. Different." He squeezes my hand. "I don't have all the answers, but what I do know is that I was given a second chance. And now I have to figure out what to do with it."

It is all so Oprah-esque. So un-Jeremy. But I squeeze back, feel the bones of his hand, the smooth bumps of his knuckles. "I'm just glad you're okay," I whisper. I can't take my eyes off his face: the dark hair, the high sharp cheekbones, the ridiculously thick dark eyelashes. Nothing has changed and everything has changed. I feel like there are a million miles between us.

≈

Back home, I help Bill make dinner while Vicky talks on the phone to her friend Hanna, another volunteer from her prison group. "We do what we can," Vicky is saying. "We can't control the outcome, Hanna."

The outcome, presumably, being that eventually pretty much everyone on death row gets executed. Vicky spends an awful lot of her time supporting the other volunteers. Trying to help them see that what they do is worthwhile. That it makes a difference.

"Mel, can you make the sauce?" Bill slides the cookbook across the counter to me. You can tell which recipes we always use because the pages are all stained. Peanut sauce is a staple; it even makes broccoli taste good. I pull peanut butter and soy sauce out of the cupboard and rummage in the fridge in hopes of finding cilantro.

"Vicky said you saw Jeremy today." He reaches past me and picks up a jar of crushed garlic. "How is he? Spirits, I mean, not ribs?"

"Good," I say, finding the cilantro—past its prime but salvageable. "Weirdly good though."

"How so?"

I pinch off the stems and rinse the green leaves, picking off the slimy bits. "Like, he thinks it happened for a reason. I mean, that he survived for a reason."

Bill nodded. "Trying to make sense of it."

"Yeah, but..." I shrug, exasperated. "It's not like there's some master plan here."

"My atheist daughter," Bill says. "You've always been a skeptic. Never even bought into the Santa Claus thing."

"Come on," I say. "You don't think someone reached down and said, 'Oh look, someone jumping off a bridge. I think I'll save this one.'"

"Nope. You know I don't." He laughs. "Skepticism runs in the family."

"Well then." I start chopping the cilantro with unnecessary vigor.

"But it doesn't much matter what we think." Bill leans back against the counter, watching me with a thoughtful expression. "Maybe it's helpful for him to believe that."

"Maybe," I say. "It just seems like a cop-out, you know?"

"How so?"

"Like, two days ago, life sucked so much he wanted to die. And now, it's like all his problems are gone and he's happier than he's been since I've known him." I look up at him. "You know? It doesn't make sense."

He nods. "Life sometimes doesn't."

"Then shouldn't we just, I don't know, accept that? Not go making stuff up to make ourselves feel better?"

"Hmm." Bill shakes his head. "Why so angry, Mel?"

"I'm not angry!" I realize I'm almost shouting and try to lower my voice. "Well, maybe I am. I don't know. Maybe I'm angry that my best friend jumped off a f…freaking bridge."

"You can call it a fucking bridge if you want," he says. "Not like I haven't heard it before. Actually, it's not like I haven't said it before."

I slap the knife down on the chopping board. "I'm not hungry," I say. "I'm going up to my room."

Bill just nods. "Do what you need to do."

I stomp upstairs, hating him for being so reasonable. I want to scream at someone, but getting mad at my father is useless. It just ends up making me feel worse. It makes me think about Jeremy and his father and the disastrous afternoon in Jacksonville and how it was the final straw that sent us driving to the bridge that same night.

Like everything else, it was my fault.

Execution Day

After Jeremy told me about his father that day at the beach, I couldn't stop thinking about him. It just seemed impossible to me that his father wouldn't want to see him. I mean, he'd lost Lucas. Jeremy was all he had. And yet it had been almost a year since Jeremy had seen his father. They hadn't even spoken.

It made no sense at all.

And then there was Ramon, whose execution was coming up fast. Unless there was a last-minute miracle, he'd be given a lethal injection and that would be it: life over. Mom had told me that his daughter had come up from Miami to visit again, knowing this would be the last time she saw him alive. She wasn't planning to come for the execution. She didn't want to watch that, and I couldn't blame her.

Mom hadn't met Ramon; her advocacy was more arm's length—petitions, the website, letter writing, meetings with politicians. Her friend Hanna had formed a close friendship with Ramon, though, visiting as often as she could. Hanna had told me that Ramon's greatest regret was that he wouldn't get to see his daughter grow up.

And Jeremy's dad, who had that opportunity, was just throwing it away.

It made me furious, and I couldn't let it go.

After school on Tuesday, Jeremy and I hung out at the park near my house. We were sitting on the high wooden platform of the old playground equipment—faded blue-and-red plastic slide, rusting monkey bars and a five-foot-high climbing wall. I debated rolling a cigarette and then remembered I had given Jeremy my tobacco and was supposed to have quit. I didn't think I was addicted, exactly, but I missed the ritual of it, the feel of the thin paper and loose tobacco compressing between my fingertips.

Jeremy stretched out on his back and put his head on my lap. We still weren't exactly going out—we hadn't even kissed yet—but we seemed to be heading in that direction. Maybe. I wanted to be with him all the time, but I wasn't sure if I wanted to risk the friendship by trying to turn it into something more. I pushed the thought away. "Jer?"

"Mmm."

"I was thinking about what you said. About your dad." I could feel his spine stiffen. "Maybe he's scared to make the first move, you know?"

He raised his eyebrows, and I felt my cheeks heat up. I wished I'd used some other expression. "I mean, maybe he thinks you're angry with him."

"Yeah, well, he'd be right."

"I know—I mean, you have a right to be. But maybe he's waiting for you to get in touch with him."

Jeremy sat up. "You think I should make the first move, huh?"

I nodded.

"You sure it's my dad you're talking about here?"

"What?" My face was on fire. "Yeah, of course. What else?"

He shrugged. "I don't know. Maybe you're right."

"Yeah?"

"It's not like I haven't thought about it. You know, on and off. I know where he's living and all that. He's got an apartment in Jacksonville."

"You think you might call him?" I was still feeling flustered about what we hadn't said. Had he been *flirting* with me?

Jeremy made a face. "Too weird. What would I say?"

"I don't know. 'Hi, Dad, it's Jeremy'?"

"Yeah, but then what?" He folded his arms across his chest. "I mean, he says hi and maybe 'it's been a while' or something obvious like that. And then? I just imagine this long awkward silence."

I grimaced. "Yeah, it'd be hard to just pick up like nothing happened. I mean, you can't exactly ignore his not talking to you for a year."

"He's not much of a talker anyway," Jeremy said. "I mean, even when he was around. Before Lucas died. We weren't ever close like you and Bill, you know?"

"Yeah." Jeremy was tall and lanky and dark-haired like his mom; Lucas had been fair-haired and athletic. I wondered if he'd looked like their dad, whom I pictured as a military kind of guy, short hair and muscular build, with a tough-guy attitude.

"If I was going to do anything, I'd probably go up to Jacksonville and try and see him in person," Jeremy said.

"I'd go with you," I said. "Actually…"

"What?"

"Vicky's going up on Friday. To protest at the jail. There's an execution scheduled." I bit my lip, pushing aside a mental image of Ramon and his daughter. "Florida State Prison's not far from Jacksonville. I bet we could get a ride with her. I mean, if you want."

He shook his head. "I don't know if it's a good idea."

"Come on. What have you got to lose?"

Jeremy didn't say anything for a long minute. Finally, he looked at me, his dark eyes shining. "Maybe I don't want to find out."

≈

By the time Friday came, Jeremy had decided to come to Jacksonville with Vicky and me. The trip there was fun: we were skipping school, the sky was blue, Vicky had the tunes playing, and Jeremy came prepared with snacks.

"Gotta have road-trip food," he said, sliding into the backseat with a duffel bag. "I stopped at the Winn-Dixie."

"Whatcha got?" I asked, suddenly hungry even though I'd only just had breakfast.

He unzipped the bag and pushed it forward, wedging it between the two front seats. "Licorice allsorts, pretzels, Doritos, chili-lime peanuts…"

Vicky started to laugh. "We're driving to Jacksonville, not California."

"Chocolate?" I asked hopefully.

Jeremy passed me an Aero bar. "So, the execution is today, huh? Have you met the guy, Vicky?"

"No." She glanced at him in the rearview mirror. "Honestly, I'd find it too hard to do this work if I got to know the prisoners. My friend Hanna is going to have a rough time, I think. She keeps saying what a good guy Ramon is."

"Mmm. Will she be there?"

"Not watching, but yeah, outside with us. Well, with me." She took a sip of the coffee in her travel mug. "You guys are going to do your own thing, right? Head in to Jacksonville, do some shopping or whatever?"

I waited to see what Jeremy was going to say. I wouldn't have been surprised if he told her the whole story—people often did with Vicky. He just shrugged though. "Yeah, we'll check out the scene at the prison with you and then we'll head downtown."

"You're welcome to take the car," Vicky said. "Just make sure you come back for me. Or call. If you want to take the car and go home sooner, I can probably get a ride with Hanna. She drove up yesterday so she could see Ramon."

"What time is…I mean, will they announce when they've done it? Executed him?" I fumbled with my words.

"Scheduled for six thirty."

"I guess he'll have his last meal?" Jeremy asked.

"Cheeseburger, fries, onion rings, coleslaw, chocolate cake and a pint of Ben & Jerry's ice cream."

I stared at her. "And you know this how?"

"Twitter," she said. "Believe it or not."

≈

Shortly before noon, we arrived at the prison, parked and walked to a big grassy area outside, where a number of people were gathered. There was a group of maybe ten people sitting near a table with photographs of a young black man—Michael Daniels, one of the two men that Ramon had killed. His family and friends, I figured, waiting to hear that Ramon was finally dead. Some had lawn chairs and coolers—I guessed it made sense if you were going to be there all day, but it seemed weird. "Execution-day picnic," Jeremy muttered in my ear.

I looked at the group. One person caught my eye—a frail-looking black woman in a wheelchair. She looked about sixty, her hair gray and tightly scraped back off a thin face. I wondered if she was Michael's mother and if she'd been waiting sixteen years for the day her son's murderer would be killed. I wondered how she felt about it, and whether she ever thought of Ramon as a person, and if she knew he had a daughter. I wondered how she'd feel at the end of the day, going home after the execution. Killing Ramon wasn't going to bring her son back.

Standing a respectful distance away was a group of death-penalty protesters, many of whom I recognized from various events over the years: Vicky's friend Pam, who did the website stuff; Hanna, dressed in black, her long red hair tied back in a ponytail; Pete and Gary, a gay couple who, I knew from Vicky, were trying to adopt a brother and sister currently in foster care; and a bearded college professor whose name I'd forgotten. A woman

I didn't recognize was carrying a poster—*Gainesville Citizens Against the Death Penalty*—and smoking a cigarette. There were some younger people too, university students, probably, many of them holding protest signs: *REPEAL THE DEATH PENALTY! TWO WRONGS DON'T MAKE A RIGHT. KILLING IS ALWAYS WRONG.*

There were death-penalty supporters too. As we approached, an older man with a red face waved his sign at me. *THE WAGES OF SIN ARE DEATH* was painted in drippy red letters. I shuddered and stepped around him, avoiding eye contact.

"Bit bloodthirsty, isn't it?" Jeremy whispered.

I nodded, looking at the faces and the signs. *An eye for an eye. Burn in hell, sinners.* All that certainty and anger and self-righteousness. Who were these people for whom life was so black and white? So uncomplicated? It made me think about people being run out of town, of mobs and lynchings. Maybe these were the people who, back in those days, would have been exacting their own form of justice.

"So everyone just waits?" Jeremy said.

Vicky nodded. "Basically, yeah. Our presence is a way of saying that we are aware of what happens inside those walls. That we care. That these deaths aren't going unnoticed."

Jeremy shook his head. "Crazy."

I thought I knew what he meant. There was a man inside that building who, in just a few hours, would be killed. He would be strapped down on a gurney, a needle would be jabbed into a vein in his arm, and a lethal dose of drugs would be delivered until his heart stopped beating. And this murder was all legal, accepted, authorized by our government and supported by our fellow Americans. It seemed like we should be storming the building, screaming, fighting. There should be outrage. Instead, we had this handful of people with their polite signs. It was beyond inadequate.

Vicky looked at me as if she knew exactly what I was thinking. "It does make a difference, Mel."

"Yeah, but you have to think that," I said.

"Look at the opposition to what we do. People wouldn't react so strongly if they thought we were powerless to make change." She turned to Jeremy. "You wouldn't believe the phone calls we get. One time when I was here for an execution, someone drove by and shouted at me that he hoped someone murdered my kids so I could see how that felt. And then he threw a bag of dog shit at me."

I remembered it well. Vicky had come home in tears, shaking from head to toe.

"That's disgusting." Jeremy grimaced and looked around at the small group of protesters. "I hope nothing like that happens today."

She shrugged. "We'll be fine. I just take it as evidence that we must be doing something right."

Jeremy shook his head and turned to me. "You want to hang around a bit? Or…"

Hanging around the prison was the last thing I wanted to do. I shook my head. "Let's get out of here."

My mother studied me with that measured, concerned look in her eyes. "Are you okay, Mel?"

"Yeah. But would you mind if we didn't come back after all? You said you could get a ride, right?"

Vicky nodded. "Absolutely, Mel. I'll get a ride home with Hanna, or Pam's here too." She tilted her head and smiled at me. "I think you two should just go and have some fun."

Last Meal

It only took us half an hour to find Jeremy's dad's address in southwest Jacksonville. It was a small gray apartment building on a busy street, and it had a definite rental look to it—not ugly, just impersonal and bland.

Jeremy pulled into a parking spot out in front. "Well, here we are."

"You want me to wait out here?"

He shrugged. "He's probably not even home."

"Only one way to find out," I said. My stomach was queasy and unsettled, whether because of Ramon or Jeremy's father, I wasn't sure.

"Right." He didn't move though. "I had another dream about my brother last night."

"You did? Could you talk to him?" I always trod carefully around this subject, because talking about dreams was the closest we'd come to arguing. I'd read some of the stuff he'd sent me, but it seemed kind of hokey. To me,

142

dreams were just our brains doing nightly maintenance, neurons firing up a random mix of whatever we'd been doing or thinking about—but I knew that to Jeremy they were something much more serious.

"He was at the beach, you know? Where I showed you; where it happened? Standing there in his shorts, holding the volleyball that Daimon and Carter had been playing with. I walked up to him and called out his name…" He shook his head. "And he stayed there, just staring at me, not smiling or anything. Just staring."

"And?"

"I asked him if he was okay. I knew I was dreaming, Mel. It was totally a lucid dream. I told him that…" His voice broke. "I said I was sorry."

I wanted to reach across and touch him, put my hand on his arm maybe, but I didn't do it. "Did he respond?"

He shook his head. "No. He just turned and walked away. I ran after him, but he ran into the water and started swimming away from shore. And I swam too, but I couldn't catch him, and then there was all this seaweed grabbing my ankles and pulling me under…and I couldn't breathe…and I woke up coughing and choking." He shuddered. "It was horrible."

"Kind of turned into a nightmare, it sounds like."

"I think maybe he was punishing me, you know? That he wanted me to know what it felt like to drown."

I shook my head helplessly. "You're punishing yourself. I mean, it's not him, it's you. You're torturing yourself, Jeremy."

"No. I was willing him to answer me, to talk to me. And up until then, I was in control of the dream." Jeremy looked at me, his dark eyes locked on mine. "He refused to speak to me, Mel. He took over."

"It was a dream," I said. "Just a dream."

"He'll never forgive me," Jeremy said, and in his voice I could hear his hopelessness. I could feel the powerful gravity of his guilt, sucking everything in, like one of Suzy's black holes.

"He can't," I said flatly. "He's gone, Jeremy. He's dead. You have to forgive yourself."

He snorted. "Thanks, Oprah."

I flushed. "That's not fair."

"Life isn't fair—" He broke off. "That's my dad. Crap." He ducked his head. "I don't want him to see me."

"That guy?" A tall man with short fair hair had just walked out the front doors of the building and was heading down the path toward our car.

"Crap, crap, crap." Jeremy started the engine and hit the gas, peeling out with a screech of tires.

"Jeremy!"

"I can't do this." His voice was panicky.

I glanced over my shoulder. The man was walking along the sidewalk, heading away from us. "Are you sure?"

"Yes. God. Did he see us, do you think?"

"No. He didn't even look our way."

Jeremy turned onto a side street and pulled over. "I'm sorry, Mel. I'm fucked up. I mean, I kind of dragged you all this way."

"I don't care about that," I said. "But are you really sure you don't want to talk to him?"

He leaned against the steering wheel, head on his arms. I could see his shoulders shaking slightly. I put a hand on his back, feeling the knobs of his spine through his thin cotton shirt. "You don't have to. I mean, you should just do whatever you want."

Jeremy muttered something I couldn't quite hear.

"What?"

"I said, I'm such a fucking coward."

"You're not," I protested. "What you've been through… anyone would have trouble dealing with it."

He didn't say anything.

"You can talk to me," I whispered. "If you want to."

"Nothing to say."

We sat there for a few minutes, Jeremy's face hidden in his arms, me stroking his back softly and waiting. The clock on the dashboard flashed the minutes ticking away, and my mind kept wandering back to the jail, to Ramon watching those same minutes tick away: 1:12, 1:13, 1:14… I couldn't imagine what it would be like to know you had less than six hours left to live.

"I was thinking about the Skyway Bridge thing," Jeremy said, his head still down and his voice muffled by his arms.

"Yeah?" We hadn't talked about it for a while.

"Maybe we should just do it, you know? Just jump off and be done with this."

"I know," I said. "The world is a pretty shitty place."

Jeremy sat up, ran his hand through his hair and blew out a long breath. "Sorry to be such a basket case," he said.

"Forget it," I said. His eyes were all red and bloodshot. "Remember when we first met? And talked about Camus?"

"Yeah, I remember."

"And you said you didn't get it, how the character in the story didn't really react to his mother's death?"

Jeremy nodded.

"That's kind of how I feel sometimes," I said. "Like, you crying and being emotional about your brother— that seems right to me. Normal. But I sometimes think I don't feel emotions properly. Like, I have to fake it. Or I don't know what to feel."

"What do you mean?"

"This execution, you know? I don't feel sad or anything. Just weird."

"Well, it's not like you know the guy."

I nodded. "I know. But...Vicky cries at movies. She cries over books. I never do. Even when Bill's mother—my grandma—died, I just felt kind of empty."

"Remember that note I wrote you?" Jeremy asked. "*Since we're all going to die, it's obvious that when and how don't matter.*"

"Yeah." I hesitated. "It's not just something philosophical though. I mean, it's like I'm just shallow. Like I don't have proper emotions." It was true: even while he was sitting there crying, I didn't feel empathy exactly. After a minute or two, I felt kind of bored and impatient, and then I thought about Ramon instead. And when Jeremy chose not to talk to his dad, I didn't really feel sad for him. I mostly just felt disappointed that I wouldn't find out what was going to happen. Which seemed so wrong.

"Let's do it tonight," Jeremy said.

"Do we get a last meal?"

"Of course." He looked at me. "What would you like?"

I shrugged. "I don't know. Chocolate cheesecake."

He laughed. "How about I take you out for dinner?"

"Tonight? Really?"

"Yeah. Someplace fancy." He tilted his head. "Okay? Is it a date?"

I swallowed. "Yeah. It's a date."

Jeremy grinned at me as we pulled away from Jacksonville, and I felt my tension slip away. We ate junk food and laughed and joked all the way back to St. Pete. I wondered if he regretted not talking to his dad, but I didn't want to spoil the mood by asking. "Still on for dinner?" I asked. "Or are you too full of Doritos?"

"I'm never too full to eat," Jeremy said. "Seriously."

I laughed. "You're so skinny."

"I know, I know." He made a face. "You try growing twelve inches in, like, two years. I've been starving since ninth grade."

Jeremy drove me home and waited downstairs while I changed for dinner. I didn't know where we were going, but he'd said somewhere fancy, and even though he said I looked fine, and he wasn't planning to change out of his khakis, I didn't think jeans and a T-shirt counted as appropriate attire for a nice restaurant—or a first date.

Which this was, kind of. There was something electric in the air between us, a new tension bleeding into our usual comfortable familiarity. I brushed mascara on my lashes, smoothed on tinted lip gloss, exchanged my faded jeans for a sleeveless black dress and my runners for knee-high black boots. I studied my reflection in the mirror. I hardly ever dressed up, and I felt like I was looking at a stranger. I looked good though—my arms and shoulders were still tanned from summer, and with this dress, my short hair looked less boyish and almost chic. Probably I should have replaced my silver studs with dangly earrings or at least put on a necklace, but I didn't want to look like I was trying too hard. I blew out an unsteady breath and went downstairs.

Jeremy stood up, looked me up and down and whistled. "Look at you! Wow."

"Yeah, bit different, huh?" I folded my arms across my chest self-consciously.

"You look beautiful."

My cheeks were on fire. "So. Where are we going?"

"Ah." He raised one eyebrow. "I thought I'd surprise you."

Jeremy drove my mom's car to the restaurant because he didn't want to go home and risk having to talk to his mom. "It'd be too weird," he said. "You know what I mean?"

I didn't really. "Us going to dinner?"

"No. Well, yes, but more just knowing that…" He trailed off. "I don't know. Forget it."

I raised an eyebrow. "Whatever you want. Vicky won't care if we take her car."

"Good." He drove quickly, aggressively, weaving in and out of traffic.

"Take it easy," I said mildly. "I'd like to survive the drive."

Jeremy laughed, took one hand off the steering wheel and lowered it to my bare knee. I caught my breath and put my hand on top of his. He winked at me. "Wouldn't it be ironic, getting killed in a car accident on your way to your last meal?"

I wished he'd drop the last-meal stuff. I felt like things were just beginning.

We parked in front of the Vinoy Renaissance Resort, home of Marchand's. Only one of the fanciest restaurants in St. Pete. "No way," I said.

"Why not?" Jeremy got out of the car and came around to my side, taking my arm like we were in some old-fashioned movie. "Are you taller than usual?"

I laughed and lifted one foot for his inspection. "I almost never wear heels. I got these during that brief goth period I told you about."

"Hmm." He looked at me thoughtfully. "Death Wish."

I wrinkled my nose. "Don't call me that." Our faces were only inches apart, and I lifted mine toward his. *Kiss me, kiss me, kiss me.*

Jeremy placed both his hands on my cheeks, cupping my face gently. "Melody."

"Yes."

"You...I hope you know...The thing is, I really..." His voice trailed off. "I mean, I want you to know that I...well..."

I started to laugh. Maybe it wasn't very romantic of me, but I couldn't help it. He looked so terribly earnest, and he could barely string two words together. "Are you going to kiss me or what?" I whispered.

"I'm going to kiss you," he said.

"Good."

"So stop talking."

"Okay." Then Jeremy's lips were on mine, his hands still holding my face, and I could hardly breathe. I put my hands on his shoulders, holding on to him, and I felt for a moment as if we were one person, like the boundaries between us were blurring, like his breath was in my lungs and his heartbeat was racing in my body. I slid one of my hands across his collarbone, onto his thin hard chest, and found the steady thumping of his heart. His lips parted, his tongue touching mine, and his mouth tasted like mint and something sweet, licorice maybe.

I'd kissed a few guys and done a bit more than that with a couple of them, but I'd never felt like this. I was melting. "Jeremy…"

"Mel." He pulled back, watching me with those dark eyes. "Are you…is this okay?"

"Better than okay," I said.

It took us a while, but eventually we managed to pull ourselves apart and stumble into the restaurant. The lights were too bright and the tablecloths too white, and everything was making me giggle. "I feel like I'm drunk," I whispered.

Jeremy nodded, grinning goofily at me. His eyes looked as glazed as mine felt.

"Do you have a reservation?"

We turned our attention to the tuxedo-clad waiter. "Um, no…"

"I'm afraid we're booked until nine o'clock," he said.

"Oh." Jeremy looked embarrassed.

"It doesn't matter," I said. "We can go somewhere else."

"I wanted this evening to be perfect."

"It is." I grabbed his hand and pulled him toward the door. "It is perfect."

"I should have thought of that. Needing a reservation."

"Who cares? Come on, let's go in there." I pointed across the street, where a sign read *Delia's Café*.

"That's a coffee shop," he said.

"I bet they have cheesecake."

"I was planning on having steak," Jeremy said.

"You're a vegetarian!"

"Yeah. Last meal, though, I figured…"

"Cut that out," I said.

He shrugged. "Fine. Cheesecake it is."

A few minutes later we were sitting across from each other at a tiny corner table, sharing an enormous slab of chocolate-hazelnut cheesecake and drinking cappuccinos.

I just wanted to kiss him again, but the whole business of not having a reservation seemed to have thrown him off in a weird way. "You okay?" I asked.

"Yeah. Just, you know, distracted." He shook his head. "It's been a strange day."

I nodded, remembering watching his dad walk away and listening to Jeremy's stifled crying. And then I glanced at my watch. It was past six o'clock. Sometime in the last few minutes, while we were kissing or walking into that restaurant or talking about cheesecake, Ramon was being strapped down on a gurney in the death chamber.

A wave of nausea swept over me, and I pushed the cheesecake away. "I'm not really hungry," I said.

Jeremy took a bite, chewed, swallowed. "Yeah. Me neither."

We sat there in silence for a minute. I pushed away thoughts of Ramon and focused on Jeremy—reliving the kiss, the feeling of his lips on mine, the melting inside me—and wished we were alone together, somewhere private. "You want to just go?" I asked. "Get out of here?" I met his eyes for a second and looked away, feeling like he must know what I was thinking.

"Yeah," he said. "Let's go." He took my hand, and we walked to the car.

But instead of turning onto the highway toward my house, he turned the other way. Onto the Skyway Bridge.

That was when I realized that the song that was playing was the Clash: "Lose This Skin."

He was playing our suicide playlist.

And even then—even with it all spelled out for me so obviously that a six-year-old could have seen it—I still didn't think he was serious.

I didn't get it until he was stopping the car on the bridge, turning off the engine and getting out. And by then, it was too late. I couldn't admit that I'd never really meant to go through with it, that I'd thought it was all some childish game of make-believe. So there I was, torn between my pride and my fear, taking Jeremy's hand and leaning out over the wall, high above the dark water.

I wish more than anything that I could go back and do everything differently.

Weirdo, Freak, Retard

After leaving Jeremy at the hospital and having that stupid argument with my dad about Jeremy's weirdly good mood and his whole idea that he was saved for a reason, I want to sulk in my room for the rest of the night. I get five minutes before Bill is knocking on my door.

"What?" My tone is snappish and I don't care.

"Don't forget you're babysitting Suzy," he says through the door.

"I know." *Crap. Crap, crap, crap.* I had totally forgotten.

"I can drive you," Bill says.

"Okay." I listen for his footsteps thumping down the stairs. Then I brush my teeth, run my fingers through my hair, grab my iPad in case Suzy actually goes to sleep while I am still there, and head downstairs.

Bill drives me to Suzy's house. Nina greets me warmly at the front door—and she acts so normal that I can tell she doesn't know about Jeremy. There are cookies on the kitchen table, and Suzy is curled up on the couch with her laptop.

"I'll be back by ten," Nina says, zipping her tall leather boots. "I've just told Suzy ten more minutes on the computer, so make sure she gets off. She's been staring at a screen for over an hour already."

"Okay. Have fun." As she walks out the door, I remember that she's meeting a friend who's in some kind of crisis, so probably *fun* was the wrong word. I open my mouth and then close it again as she shuts the door behind her.

"Mom?" Suzy looks up. "Oh. Mel. What are you doing here?"

"Babysitting," I say. "Your mom just left."

"Oh. She did?"

"She said bye to you," I tell her. "And you said bye back to her."

"No I didn't."

"Yeah, you did, actually."

Her brow furrows, and a sharp warning note edges into her voice. "Maybe you think you heard that, but you're wrong. I'd know if I said something."

This is typical Suzy. She's super smart, but her brain is always doing something else, so she's only ever half present. I know better than to argue with her though. "Whatcha working on?" I ask instead.

"Oh, it's just the NASA website. Want to see? You can see the latest pictures the Hubble has taken. See this? That's the Horsehead Nebula."

"Cool." I sit down beside her and look at the image on her screen. A dark cloud the shape of a horse's head, set against a reddish glow. Bursts of color, swirls of light in the darkness of space. She zooms in on something. "See that? That's Sigma Orionis. Cool, huh?"

All I can think about is Jeremy. Lying there in his hospital bed, telling me how this was all meant to be. How *happy* he was now that he'd jumped off a bridge.

"Mel! You're not paying attention."

"Sorry. What?"

"Nothing," she says sulkily. "Forget it."

My eyes are suddenly stinging with tears that I don't want Suzy to see. I mumble something about needing to pee, get up and lock myself in the washroom. Then I sit on the edge of the bathtub and let myself cry.

Jeremy might be happy now, but I can't imagine ever feeling okay again.

≈

I've washed my face and redone my eyeliner, but when I come out of the bathroom, Suzy looks up from the computer screen and narrows her eyes like she can see right through me. "What took you so long?"

"Nothing," I say. "You should get off the computer. Your mom said ten minutes."

"In a second," she says. "I'm almost done."

"Not in a minute," I say irritably. "Now."

Suzy slams the laptop closed. "There! Are you happy now?"

"It's just that your mom said—"

"I was right in the middle of something!" Her face flushes pink, and her eyes fill with tears. "Why can't you just let me be? Now I'll have to start over!"

"Sorry," I say. "I didn't realize—"

"You didn't ask! Why are you being so mean?" Her voice is loud; she's right on the edge of an angry sobbing meltdown, and I know from experience that once she slips over that edge, it can take hours to get her back.

"Suzy, I really am sorry. I've had a rough day, and I was impatient." I hesitate, not sure whether asking her what she was working on will help or make things worse. I don't have the energy to cope with a tantrumming eight-year-old. "Can I help you with whatever it is you were doing?"

"Not if I'm not allowed on the computer," she says.

"How long would it take?"

"You wouldn't understand it anyway." Fierce and certain and self-righteous.

"I could try."

"It'd take too long to explain." She's still angry, but she is calming down, the blotchy red fading from her cheeks. "I was looking forward to you coming, but you're not being very fun."

Yeah, because my best friend just tried to kill himself. I take a deep breath and swallow the words and my own anger. Sometimes I have to remind myself that she is just a kid. Eight years old. It's hard to remember that when she talks like an adult and argues like a lawyer and knows more about science than most high school students. If she was more typical—playing with dolls and plastic ponies and talking about whatever TV shows most third-graders watch—her self-centeredness would seem entirely normal. "Suzy, I'm sorry," I say. "I always look forward to seeing you too."

She sniffs and rubs her eyes with two small fists. Her nails, and a fair bit of fingertip skin, are painted dark blue with sparkles—the same polish she used on my nails the last time she did them. Nail polish is one of the very few girly things she likes.

"Want to do my nails?" I offer. "See, I've chipped most of it off."

She nods.

"And tell me about how school's going," I suggest.

Suzy stands up. "I'll do your nails," she says. "But I don't want to talk about school."

We sit on the floor in her room, a towel spread out under us to protect the carpet—Suzy is the clumsiest kid I've ever met and has yet to do my nails without dripping polish, dropping the brush or knocking over the bottle—and the whole story of her week spills out, as I figured it would. Apparently, some girls have been teasing her, calling her names—the worst of which is Poo.

"Poo?" I ask. "That's a little strange."

"Suzy, then Suzy Poozie, then Poozie. Then Fen started calling me Poo, and Emma and Danielle and everyone else joined in."

"So call them something back," I suggest. "Fen Feces. Emma Excrement."

She giggles, and the nail-polish brush veers a little wildly across my thumbnail.

"Danielle Diarrhea."

A snort and a full-on laugh. "Connie Constipation," she says. "Shonna Shithead."

"Suzy!" I'm guessing her mom and her teacher are going to love me for this line of defense.

She stops laughing. "I'd just end up getting in trouble," she says. "Anyway, they'd just call me other stuff. Like weirdo or freak or retard."

"They call you retard?"

Suzy doesn't say anything right away. She paints the nail of my index finger, my ring finger, my pinkie.

Then she puts the brush back in the bottle, screws it tight and shakes it vigorously. "One girl asked if I have some kind of mental problem," she says, not looking at me.

I remember Jeremy talking about how he was teased at school, how he used to spin in circles and how the teachers thought he was autistic. "Kids are all different," I tell her. "There's nothing wrong with you. Anyway, even if you did have some kind of problem, no one should call you names, right?"

"There's a boy in my class who has autism," Suzy says. She holds the nail-polish bottle up to the light and studies it, like she's trying to see through it or something. "He's nice and he's smart."

"Right," I say. "Well, you're pretty nice and smart yourself." I wonder if she is noticing how different she is, trying to make sense of it somehow, looking for an explanation.

"You want me to do your other hand?"

"If you want to."

Suzy unscrews the bottle top and starts painting the nails of my left hand. "We sometimes talk at lunchtime, but I think maybe I shouldn't hang out with him anymore," she says. Her cheeks are red and blotchy again. "I don't want to make him feel bad, but maybe if I didn't talk to him, the girls wouldn't be so mean to me?"

I don't know what to tell her. I want her to be brave and stand up to the girls and be loyal to her friend, but maybe that is too much to ask of an eight-year-old. "What do you think?" I say at last. "How would you feel if you did that?"

"Bad."

"It's a tough situation," I say, watching the tiny brush stroking my nails with its sparkly dark blue. "It'll get better, Suzy. As you get older. You'll find people who are more like you, and other kids will stop being so mean."

"When? I mean, how much older?"

I shrug, thinking of last year and all the stuff I went through with Devika and Adriana. "I don't know," I say. "High school will probably be better. I mean, some kids will still be jerks, but it's not so bad if you at least have one good friend. Someone who gets you."

She stops painting my nails, brush hovering, dripping, in midair, and looks up at me. "Like Jeremy?"

I have to turn away from her small face, her wide, hopeful eyes. "Yeah. Like Jeremy," I say.

The Point of It All

The next day, I smile at Adriana when I pass her in the cafeteria. I don't really mean to—it just happens, as much from nervousness as anything, but the smile she flashes back is wide and grateful and, well, genuine. I've tried not to think about that party and what I did, but now I'm questioning everything. Had she tried to save my life? Was taking those pills really a suicide attempt? It seemed like everyone else had seen it as one, even though I was pretty sure I never intended to die. Although, look at Jeremy—jumping and then realizing, too late, that he wanted to live. No one could say he hadn't attempted suicide, but maybe the only difference was that it's a lot easier to stop after five Tylenol than when you're falling from a bridge.

I'll talk to her, I decide. Apologize, or accept her apology, or whatever. I don't think we'll be friends again, not like we used to be, but it'd be a relief not to feel like we're enemies. I grab a salad and an iced tea and carry my tray toward her table. She's sitting with Devika and some other girls I don't know. Devika looks up, her perfect dark eyebrows raised in surprise, and I lose my nerve. I drop my eyes and walk past.

I am such a coward.

==

Jeremy texts me every few minutes all afternoon.

Come see me.

Dying of boredom.

Ribs hurt. Ouch.

Guess what? Still bored.

Can you come after school?

Hey had the weirdest dream. Tell you later.

The thing is, I don't know if I want to hear about his dreams anymore. I feel like his dreams were part of the problem; his dreams made him believe his brother was out there somewhere, waiting for him. And Jeremy may be able to say he's dying of boredom, like that's a normal thing to say, but just seeing the word *dying* makes me flinch. And I can't help wondering what he thinks of me now. Does he know I was never really serious about jumping? Or does he think I changed my mind, or lost my nerve?

And what about that kiss? Was that only because he wanted to do it before he died? Does it still mean anything now that he wants to live?

Couldn't text in math, I reply between classes. Can't come tonight—too much homework.

His reply is instant. How about tomorrow?

I don't know why I want to avoid him. Yes I do: just thinking about him makes me feel guilty and messed up. OK tomorrow is good. Right after school.

Can't wait to see you. Can't wait to see you ☺

I stare at the screen of my phone. Jeremy has just used a happy-face emoticon. It's like his whole personality has changed.

≈

"Not going to see Jeremy tonight?" Bill asks as we are all sitting down for dinner.

I shake my head. "Tons of homework. I told him I'd come tomorrow."

"I see." He pours himself a glass of ice water from the pitcher and takes a sip.

"How is he?" Vicky asks.

"Bored," I say. "Sore."

"His poor mother," Vicky says. "I can't imagine what she must be going through. Do you know her well, Mel?"

I shake my head. "Not at all. I mean, I've met her a couple of times but just briefly."

"I was wondering if I should call her," Vicky muses. "I don't want to intrude though."

"She's kind of formal," I say. "Not a relaxed kind of person. Their house is, like, perfect, you know?"

"Well, she's lost a lot, hasn't she? Her younger son dying and her husband leaving." Vicky piles salad onto her plate and drowns it in blue-cheese dressing. "So maybe having the house perfect helps her feel in control."

"Please," I say. "You haven't even met the woman, so don't start psychoanalyzing her."

"I'm not. Well, I didn't mean to. I just meant don't judge."

"I wasn't judging," I say. "If anyone was judging, you were. All I said was that her house is perfect."

Bill lets out an exaggerated sigh. "You two. Enough."

I look down at my plate.

"Would it bother you if I called her?" Vicky asks. "Because if you would rather I didn't…"

"Do what you want," I say.

And then the phone rings. I jump up to answer it. Vicky and Bill don't answer the phone if they're busy—and busy includes not just stuff like eating dinner, but things like reading a book or watering the plants—

but I can't let it ring. I always think it might be important, even though half the time it's only someone trying to sell carpet-cleaning services or vacation scams.

"Hello?"

"Is that Melanie?"

"Um, Melody. Yes."

"It's Mrs. Weathers."

Weird timing. "Um, hi. Is Jeremy okay?"

"He's doing well. The doctor says he should be able to come home by the end of the week."

"That's great!"

"Yes." She doesn't sound convinced. "I've spoken to the school and they're pulling together some homework for him. I was wondering if you'd be able to bring it when you visit tomorrow."

"Sure. Do I just get it from the office?"

"Yes. That would be a big help." She hesitates. "He says he doesn't want to go back to school. Do you know if… was there anything happening at school that I should know about?"

"You mean like bullying or something? I don't think so."

"Well. Maybe you can talk to him."

"Sure." He'd better come back. School would really suck without Jeremy there.

"Thank you, Melody. I know you are very important to him."

It has the ring of a question. Like, *are you his girlfriend?* I wish I knew the answer.

≈

The next day after school, I show up at the hospital with an armload of books and papers from Jeremy's teachers.

"Ah, let me guess. My mom called you."

"Yeah. This is from Mr. Daniels, and this is—"

He cuts me off. "Just put them over there," he says, sitting up and nodding toward the table in the corner. "I told her I'm not going back, but she doesn't want to hear it."

I dump the books and take a seat in the chair beside his bed. He's wearing regular clothes, no longer hooked up to all the tubes. "You look good. Better."

"I feel pretty good, as long as I don't move. Or cough or anything." He smiles at me. "I guess the ribs take a while to heal. You can't put a cast on them, you know?"

"Yeah." I pull my feet up onto the chair and wrap my arms around my knees. "Are you serious? About not going back to school, I mean?"

He nods. "One hundred percent."

"Like, actually quit? Drop out?"

"Yeah."

"Why? I mean, what are you going to do? You can't go to college if you don't graduate."

"I know. I just don't see the point of it all."

I stare at him. "Um, getting a degree? A decent job? Maybe even, I don't know, doing something useful."

"That's just it," he says eagerly. "I want to do something useful. I survived that fall, Mel. There has to be a reason for that. Something I'm meant to do."

I don't know what to say.

Jeremy gestures at the stack of books I delivered. "All that just seems so irrelevant now."

"Yeah? Your teachers won't think so."

"Exactly. They think all that stuff matters. That's why I can't go back, Mel. I can't sit in class and write exams and pretend that I care about a letter on a piece of paper." His eyes search mine, dark and intense, like he's trying to see right inside my head. "You understand, don't you?"

"Yeah. I guess so." It's not entirely untrue. I mean, of course I think lots of stuff about school is kind of pointless. Of course I know that I'm jumping through all kinds of hoops and that it isn't all exactly meaningful. But Jeremy and I have talked about that kind of thing since we met, and neither of us has ever considered quitting. "Will your mom let you quit?"

"I don't know," he says. "I just know I was saved for a reason."

I shake my head, feeling tears welling in my eyes. I feel like I'm losing him, like he's slipped away somehow to some other place where I can't follow him. "School's going to suck without you," I say.

Crazy Is Normal

By the weekend, Jeremy is out of hospital and back at home. He's recovered from the surgery and, medically, there's not much more the doctors can do. Apparently broken ribs take a long time to heal, like a couple of months, but all you can do is rest and take painkillers, and you don't need a hospital bed for that. I visit him on Saturday and we sit on his bed and watch a couple of movies on Netflix, but we don't talk about anything much. As long as we don't talk, I can pretend he's still the same Jeremy.

His mom hovers around, tidying and putting away laundry and basically finding excuses to come up to his room and check on us every other minute.

"Um, what's up with your mother?" I ask at last.

"Yeah, get used to that. She's taking some time off work," Jeremy says. He pauses the movie. "She's being kind of crazy, actually."

"Well, I'm sure she's worried."

"She thinks the hospital shouldn't have let me come home." He shrugs. "But the psychiatrist doesn't think I'm a risk to myself or others, so here I am."

"Are you still seeing him? I mean, is there…you know, some kind of follow-up?"

"Yeah, yeah. Mom's dragging me to various appointments." He looks at me. "I'm not going to do it again. I mean, I'm not, like, suicidal or anything. You know that, right?"

"I guess." Then again, I didn't ever think he'd do it in the first place.

"Do you still think about it?" he asks.

"No." I flash back to that moment on the bridge, watching his body drop like a stone into the darkness, and I shiver. "I couldn't do that to my parents," I say. "Even if things were really bad, I don't think I could do that to them."

"Good," he says. "It's the most selfish thing I've ever done." He reaches out and puts a hand on my arm. "I'm going to make up for it somehow. I know there's a reason that I'm still here."

Here we go again. "Let's watch the movie," I say.

When I get home that evening, Vicky is at her computer in the living room, banging away on the keys like it's an old-fashioned typewriter, and Bill is in the kitchen, cooking fish.

I wrinkle my nose. "Can we open some windows?"

"Be my guest." He chops red onion on a wooden cutting board. "How's Jeremy?"

"Fine. He says he's not going back to school though." I pick up a sliver of onion and smell it, trying to block out the fishy stink. "Which sucks."

"Mmm, yes." He nods toward Vicky. "Your mother just got some bad news. Appeal denied for one of the men on death row. Young guy—still in his thirties."

"Last appeal?"

"Yeah. Out of options. Execution date set a month from now."

"That sucks." I realize that this is what I just said about Jeremy not coming back to school. "I mean, more than sucks." I hesitate, and then the words rush out. "I don't know how she does it. Getting all involved in people's lives and then seeing them die." Again, I'm back on the bridge, the cool wind in my face, feeling Jeremy's hand slip from mine, seeing his fall in slow motion, the white oval of his face looking up at me. I catch my breath and grab on to the edge of the counter. Bill doesn't notice.

"She's something special, all right," he says. He reaches out and gives me a little push. "Go tell her dinner's ready in five, okay?"

≈

It's stupid. Jeremy's home, safe, but I'm a mess. I keep thinking about those moments on the bridge, keep seeing him fall, keep replaying in my mind all the conversations we had in the months leading up to that night. Like I'm trying to make sense of it, but I'm not getting anywhere, I'm just going round in the same fucked-up circles, and it still doesn't make any sense at all. I feel like my thoughts are wearing grooves into my brain, like they're carving their tracks a little deeper every time they trace the circle back around.

On Monday, I start crying in math class and can't stop. I mean, I really can't stop. I feel like I'm outside myself, just watching what a complete fool I am being, sitting at my desk with my nose running, gasping for breath. I end up down in Mrs. Paulsen's office, sniffling and snuffling and trying to calm down. She's sitting across from me in her armchair, muttering the occasional "there there" and "deep breaths." I stare past her at the inspirational kitten posters. There's one of a soaking-wet kitten climbing out of a toilet, with the caption *It could be worse!*

"Just tell me what you are thinking," Mrs. Paulsen says. "Whatever is going through your mind right now."

"I hope they didn't actually drop a cat in a toilet to get that picture," I choke out.

"Pardon?"

I shake my head, exhale a long, slow breath, clench my fists so tight I can feel my short nails digging into my palms. "Nothing. Sorry. I just…I'm fine. Really."

"You've been through a very traumatic event," Mrs. Paulsen says. "It's entirely normal to be affected by that. It would be more surprising if you weren't."

"I guess so." I hope everyone isn't talking about me, but I bet they are. Probably wondering if I'm going to do something crazy. Jump off a bridge. Overdose. Crazy Death Wish.

"How are you sleeping?"

"Okay."

"Eating?"

"Yeah. Fine." I can't look at her. "Um, just thinking about it a lot, mostly. Like, it's hard to stop sometimes, or it just comes into my head for no reason."

She nods. "Very normal, Melody. It can make you feel like you're going crazy, but it is absolutely normal." She leans to one side, opens a drawer in her filing cabinet and rummages around for a few minutes. "Here, take this."

I take a single page from her. Pale pink. *Reactions to Trauma* it says at the top.

She points a maroon fingernail at the list of bullet points on the page. "See? *Intrusive thoughts, re-experiencing the traumatic event.*" She smiles at me. "Normal reactions, Melody. You're not going crazy."

"Good." I rub my eyes so hard I see tiny spots of color. Crazy is normal; good to know.

"How is Jeremy? Have you seen him?"

I nod. "He's okay. Back at home now."

"And are you worried about him?"

"You mean, that he'll do it again?" I shake my head. "No. I don't think so."

Mrs. Paulsen doesn't say anything for a moment, just sits and waits to see if I will say more. I can't think of anything else to say though.

"I guess I'd better go back to class," I say. I'm already dreading the stares and the whispers.

She uncrosses her legs and nods a few times. "If there's anything you want to talk about, you can come and see me. Anytime."

Krishna Consciousness

After school, I text Jeremy and tell him I can't come over, that I have too much homework.

Do it here, he says.

Can't. 60% of socials grade on this paper.

Tomorrow?

Yes. See you then.

But I don't actually have a paper due. I just need to be alone.

Vicky is at her computer as usual, phone in one hand. She breaks off when she sees me come in. "Mel? Nina called," she says, putting her hand over her phone. "Give her a call back; she's hoping you can spend some time with Suzy soon."

"Fine," I say, but my heart sinks a little. I don't have the energy for Suzy right now. I don't even have the energy to talk to Nina. Up in my room, I open my laptop, intending to check email and Twitter.

My phone buzzes: Jeremy, texting me. Are you sure you can't come over?

Yes. Busy.

Thirty seconds later my phone rings. It's Jeremy. "Please come over? Pretty please?"

"I can't," I say, feeling guilty. "Listen, I can't really talk right now. I have to call Suzy's mom."

"Are you babysitting? Maybe I could come with you sometime. I liked that kid."

"Maybe," I say. "She doesn't know, um, about what happened."

"Duh," he says. "I'm not stupid. It's not like I'd tell her."

"I know, I know." Suzy's not stupid either though: I'd have to make up a story to explain his injuries, and I hate the thought of lying to her. "Jeremy, I really have to go," I say.

"Okay," he says. He sounds pretty down, but I push aside my worry and phone Nina.

She sounds relieved to hear from me. "Mel! I'm so glad you called. Suzy's having an awful time at school."

"Kids picking on her?"

"Yeah. Still. I met with the principal last week. Lots of talk. Zero tolerance for bullying and all that, but the bottom line is that kids are just cruel. Only so much the teachers can do."

"Poor Suzy."

"Yes."

I wait, wondering what she wants.

"We're thinking about taking her out of her after-school care program," she says. "It seems like that's where the worst of the bullying happens."

"What about your work?" I say. Jim's an engineer of some kind, and Nina is an attorney for a nonprofit agency. They're both pretty into their jobs. "I mean, she can't be home alone, right?"

"Mmm. That's the difficult part," she says. "Actually, that's why I was calling."

"You want me to look after her?"

"I know it's a lot to ask, but do you think there's any way you could do a regular couple of hours every day? I'm home by six, so if you could come from three to six…" She clears her throat. "I'd pay you the same as we usually do."

"Can I think about it?" I love Suzy, but I'm not sure I want to see her every day, or have that much of my time tied up. On the other hand, it's hard to say no when someone needs your help.

"Of course. And Melody, you don't have to entertain her. Feel free to bring your homework. She's pretty self-sufficient."

"Would I pick her up from school?" I'm trying to think how that would work, since I can't exactly double her on my bike.

"One of my neighbors has offered to do that. She picks up her son every day, so she's making the drive anyway. Her name's Diane; she'll wait here for you. But if you could just come here straight from school, you'd get here around the same time, I think."

Nina's got this all figured out. I can feel my resistance slipping away. "You think school will go better if she gets to leave at three?" I ask.

"I hope so. If it doesn't, I don't know what else to do," she says. "I had to take today off work because she just refused to go to school at all. Third time this month."

"Maybe you could homeschool," I say.

"I don't know." She sighs. "We'll take it one step at a time."

"Yeah." I blow out a long breath. "Okay," I say. "I can do it."

After a week at home, Jeremy is up and walking around, moving slowly and cautiously but definitely closer to recovered. Physically, at least. He's well enough to drive his mom's car and come over to my place.

"Are you really not ever going to come back to school?" I ask him. It's Saturday night and we're sitting on the couch in my room, drinking strawberry milkshakes Bill made. He puts all kinds of healthy stuff in them—wheat

germ and soy milk as well as the ice cream and berries—
but you'd never know from the taste.

Jeremy shakes his head. "I'm done."

"Suzy too," I tell him. "She doesn't want to go to school
anymore either."

"Yeah?" He doesn't sound all that interested. "Listen,
you feel like a road trip this weekend?"

"You're kidding, right? You just got out of the hospital."

"I'm fine, Mel. Don't fuss; I get enough of that at
home." He flicks his hands, brushing me off. "And I was
talking to someone online and she invited me to this thing
in Gainesville on Sunday night."

"What thing? Who?" *He's talking to some girl online?*
I push down a surge of something that might be jealousy.

"She's a student at the university," he says. "Anyway, I
wondered if you wanted to come with me."

"Wouldn't that be kind of awkward?"

"Huh?" He frowns at me.

"If she asked you out…um, she'd probably rather you
didn't bring me along."

He laughs and then winces, hand to his ribs. "It's not
like that. She's invited me to a Hare Krishna temple."

"A Hare Krishna temple," I repeat, almost laughing.
Then I see the defensiveness slide over his face like a mask,
and I stop smiling. "You're serious."

"Yeah. Absolutely. I've been reading a lot about it."

"Isn't that sort of a cult?"

"No more than anything else. Actually, less than Christianity. Hare Krishnas don't reject anything or anyone. They draw on Hindu traditions, but it's as much a philosophy as a religion." He takes a sip of his milkshake through a straw. "Mmm. These are good."

I'm thinking about Jeremy's obsession with lucid dreams and how messed up that made him, convinced his brother was out there somewhere waiting for him. This sounds like more of the same to me. "So you want to go to this temple thing?" I say, stalling for time. If it really is a cult, maybe I should go with him, just to keep him out of trouble. Not that I have a great track record in that department.

"Yeah. It sounds cool," he says. "They do meditation, you know? Prayer, dancing. And there's going to be some kind of vegetarian feast that sounds amazing."

"Right."

"And this girl—her name is Kamala—she volunteers with this group at the university, serving vegan lunches for next to nothing."

"You sure it's not a cult?"

He rolls his eyes. "I'll show you the website, okay? It's all totally legit. These are good people. People who want to make a difference."

"By meditating?"

"By developing their consciousness. Krishna consciousness." He looks at me earnestly. "I've been reading a lot about it, and it makes so much sense. Actually, I've been feeling really good—happy. And Kamala says that's actually one of the first signs of developing Krishna consciousness."

"I've noticed that you're happier," I say. "But Jeremy, nothing's changed. I don't see how this is going to fix anything." What I want to say is, how come you're the one that jumped off a bridge and now you're all happy and I'm the one who's having crazy crying jags in class? How come you kissed me and now it's like that never happened?

"Come with me," he says.

"I think I'm going to pass," I say. There's a lump in my throat, and I feel like I'm abandoning him, but I just can't see myself going to some temple to meditate and talk about Krishna. With a girl called Kamala. Not happening. "Listen," I say. "I was thinking about what you told me once, about being picked on in school when you were a kid."

"Yeah?"

"Suzy's going through a rough time with that now," I say. "And she thinks you're pretty cool. If you could talk to her—encourage her, you know? That might help."

"Sure. I could do that. When are you seeing her?"

"Every day after school for the next while," I say. "What day suits you? Sooner the better."

"How about Monday?"

I smile at him. "Perfect. I'll call and tell her. It'll give her something to look forward to."

———

I spend Sunday in my room, thinking about Jeremy, who is off in Gainesville, without me. I watch Hare Krishnas chanting on YouTube—*Hare Krishna, Hare Krishna, Krishna Krishna, Hare Hare; Hare Rama, Hare Rama, Rama Rama, Hare Hare*—and picture Jeremy doing the same thing. With a girl called Kamala.

The people in the videos look happy. Ecstatic, even. And the thing is, I do kind of understand where Jeremy's coming from. I mean, we all want to believe we're here for a reason, right? It's why we have religions. It's in our nature to want to make sense of our lives somehow. And Jeremy's had a lot to make sense of. His brother's death, his dad leaving. Like my dad said, maybe it's helpful to believe he was saved for a reason.

But then don't you have to believe that everything happens for a reason? That Lucas died for a reason? Or that Jeremy's dad left for a reason? Don't you just start accepting everything, including obviously fucked-up things like Ramon being executed?

I stare at the young men chanting on my laptop screen, with their shaved heads and wide smiles and half-closed eyes. Maybe if it makes Jeremy happy, if it helps him find some kind of peace, that should be enough. But I can't see how chanting *Hare Krishna* is going to help make the world a better place.

I can't see how Jeremy could convince himself that this is what he was saved for.

There's a knock on my door. "Mel?"

"Hey." It's Vicky. I turn away from my computer and swivel my chair around to face her.

"Homework?"

"No." I gesture at the screen. "Jeremy's off at some Hare Krishna thing. I was just looking it up."

She raises her eyebrows. "Really?"

"In Gainesville." And then I add, "With a girl called Kamala."

"Oh." She crosses the room and perches on the arm of my couch, right behind where I am sitting. "Which part are you upset about?"

"Who said I was upset?"

She tilts her head. "Honey. You're crying."

I touch my cheek and my fingers come away wet.

Her hand is on my shoulder, squeezing. "Sometimes I miss the days when you were small enough to sit on my lap. When I could tell you it would be okay and you'd believe me."

"Tell me anyway," I say.

"Oh, Mel." She looks me right in the eyes. "It will be okay, Mel. I don't know what okay will look like, but I know you'll get there."

"What about Jeremy?" I say, and I start crying for real. I close my eyes and see his body falling away from me into the darkness, that ghostly, half-imagined face looking back up at me. "Will he be okay?"

She stands up, wraps both arms around me and holds me close. "I hope so."

"I don't know what to do. How to help him."

"Just keep doing what you've always done," she says. "Just be his friend."

Being his friend had helped pave the road that led him to the Skyway Bridge. "I was his friend," I say, my voice muffled against her shoulder. "And look what happened."

"Oh, Mel. That was not your fault."

I don't say anything. After a long moment, Vicky says softly, "Be his friend, Mel."

"I will. I am."

"Sometimes we can't save people," she says. "No matter how much we want to."

Zombie Girl

On Monday, Adriana waves to me as I cycle across the parking lot after school. I slow down, wave, come to a stop in front of her. "Hey."

"Hey." She looks nervous. "How's your friend? Jeremy?"

"Getting better," I say.

"When's he coming back to school?"

I shrug. "I don't know if he is. He says he's not going to."

"Oh. Is he, like, worried about what people will think?"

I shake my head. "I don't think so." Though maybe he is. I would be. If I was called Death Wish for taking a few Tylenol, what would they call him? Though I haven't heard any of that. Maybe the very awfulness of what he did has stunned everyone into some kind of appalled silence.

"I was wondering," she says. "Do you want to get together sometime? Like, hang out and chat?"

Her cheeks are pink. She's scared I'll say no, maybe. "With Devika?"

"No. I mean, I can ask her if you want. But I meant just us."

I swallow. "Sure," I say. "I'm kind of busy with babysitting after school right now. But yeah, maybe sometime."

Adriana smiles, and I remember how much fun we used to have together. But you can't go back. You can't erase all the bad stuff that has happened.

≈

I ride my bike over to Suzy's place. I expect to see Nina's neighbor and her son, but it turns out Nina had to leave work for a meeting with Suzy's teacher today, so she drove her home herself. She's in her work clothes and heading back to the office, zipping up her boots and gathering her wallet and keys and briefcase as soon as I arrive, her words spilling out, as she goes, in a nonstop flurry of instructions (*dinner's in the fridge, it's chili, just heat it up in the microwave, Suzy might want spaghetti with it*) and gratitude (*thank you so much, I don't know what we'd do without you, you've been such a godsend*). She talks as fast as Suzy but without Suzy's gravity.

Nina is always smiling and laughing, even when, like now, she is flustered and rushed.

"It'll be fine," I say. "Don't worry."

She stops on the front steps, turns back to me. "Oh, and Suzy mentioned that your friend Jeremy's going to drop by for a visit. Feel free to invite him to stay for chili; there's plenty."

"Great."

"And tell him thanks, from me."

"I will."

And she's in her car, pulling out of the driveway with a wave.

≈

I find Suzy sitting at the kitchen table, frowning over her homework. "Hey, Suze."

She puts her pen down with obvious relief. "Mel! Guess what?"

"What?"

"I'm not going to after-school care anymore."

"I know." I laugh. "That's why I'm here, silly."

"When's Jeremy coming?"

"Soon," I tell her. "He said he'd be here by four. Shall we ask him to stay for dinner?"

She bounces in her seat, jumps up and hugs me for no apparent reason. It's actually more of a tackle, and I struggle not to lose my balance. "Yes! Did Mom tell you she bought ice cream for us? Rainbow sherbet."

"Nice."

"You think he'll like that?"

"I'm sure he will." I peel her off me. "Listen, when Jeremy gets here, don't give him a hug like that one, okay? He's got sore ribs."

"He does? How come?"

"He fell."

"Oh. Poor Jeremy." She doesn't sound too concerned. Or too curious, luckily. I guess kids fall down all the time. "How much longer until he comes?"

"It's almost four," I tell her. "He'll be here any minute." I nod toward the homework spread across the table. "What are you working on? Shall we get this done before he arrives?"

Suzy makes a face.

"Come on," I say. "Get it out of the way."

"It's boring."

"All the more reason to get it done fast."

Suzy rolls her eyes at me, but she picks up her pencil. "*Fine.*"

Sometimes I think she is more of a teenager than I am.

By four thirty, despite much procrastination and distraction, Suzy has finished her work. And Jeremy hasn't arrived.

"Phone him," she insists. "Remind him."

"He wouldn't forget," I say. "He's probably just running late."

"Then tell him to hurry up."

I make a face at her, pick up my phone and send him a quick text. At Suzy's. Where r u?

We wait for a minute, both of us staring at my phone, but there's no answer. U ok?

Still no answer.

"Where do you think he is?"

"I don't know." My chest is suddenly tight, and again I see him falling, dropping away from me into the darkness.

"Mel!" Suzy's staring at me.

"What?"

"You looked funny."

"Sorry. I'm just...I was just a bit worried. It's not like him to just not show up."

"Call him again," she says.

And I do. Again and again and again.

Then I call his mother. "It's probably nothing," I say. "I mean, he probably just forgot."

Her voice is tight, controlled. "I don't know where he is," she says.

"He's not answering my texts," I say. "I know he was going out last night."

"He didn't come home."

Suzy is mouthing something at me: What did she say? Is he coming? I turn away from her slightly and lower my voice. "Are you worried? I mean, has he called or anything?"

"Of course I'm worried, Melody," she snaps. "He's my son."

"I know. Sorry. I mean, that I bothered you at work." I hesitate. I want to ask her if she has called the police or anything, but I don't want to say that in front of Suzy. "I was wondering…it's not really like him to not show up. Do you think we should call someone?"

"He sent a text," she says wearily. "Last night. He said he'd be gone for a few days."

"*What*?"

"You know as much as I do, Melody." She clears her throat. "I have to go."

"If he gets in touch again, can you ask him to call me?"

Nothing. And then a dial tone. I stare at the phone in my hand. She just hung up on me.

"He isn't coming, is he," Suzy says flatly.

"No," I say. "No, he isn't coming."

"Figures." Her shoulders are hunched so high they're practically touching her ears. "Probably he has better things to do."

Like chanting Hare Krishna with Kamala. "No," I tell her. "He doesn't. He's just being stupid."

"Did you have a fight with him? Did you *break up*?"

I reach out to brush aside a lock of hair that has fallen across her face. "It's complicated." I see her frown and open her mouth to object, and I cut her off. "And I don't mean you wouldn't understand because you're a kid or anything like that. Stuff with Jeremy and me…well, it's just really, really complicated."

"Tell me," she says.

"He's been very sad lately. And confused."

"Because of his brother dying?"

I'd forgotten she knows about that. "Probably that's a really big part of it. He's got lots of mixed-up feelings, you know?" I'm about to say more—to turn it into a little pep talk on coping with difficult emotions—but she's shifting in her seat, turning away from me, and I can see that she's lost interest.

Suzy eyes the freezer. "Do you think we could have ice cream first and then have chili for dessert?"

Not sure her mom will approve, but whatever. "Sure, Suzy. I think we could do that."

I dish up two bowls of ice cream and we chat about the big bang and the latest theories about the composition of the first stars. Or, more accurately, Suzy chats, and I nod and say uh-huh a lot and think about Jeremy.

Maybe I should have more compassion, but I am so angry that I just want to scream at him. Selfish. It's taken his letting down an eight-year-old to make me see it, but everything he has done has been so incredibly selfish.

Right now, I don't even want to be his friend.

≈

For the rest of the week, I get through school somehow, babysit Suzy, eat dinner with my parents, do my homework. I feel kind of numb, like I'm navigating my days on autopilot. I chat with people in the hallway when I have to, but it feels forced and unreal—like there's a glass wall between me and everyone else. I try to act normal. A couple of times I have to hide in the bathroom because I think I might start to cry, but as soon as I'm alone the tears disappear and I'm just blank, staring at the graffiti on the cubicle wall.

I think about going to see Mrs. Paulsen, but I don't know what I'd say.

On Friday at dinner, Vicky asks about Jeremy. "You haven't seen him for a few days, have you? Is everything okay?"

I shrug, pushing an unappetizing piece of eggplant out of the stir-fry on my plate. "He's been away."

Her eyebrows lift. "Really? Where?"

I don't really want to get into it. I'm not sure why, but I feel sort of embarrassed. "Visiting a friend," I say. "In Gainesville."

"He must be feeling better?"

"I guess."

"What about you? We've hardly seen you this week."

I put my fork down. "Busy week, I guess."

"Is it going to work for you, spending so much time at Suzy's? I know you want to help out, but you can say no."

"It's fine."

"You don't want to take on too much." Bill takes a sip of wine, watching me over the rim of his glass. "Make sure you leave yourself enough time for your schoolwork."

I stare at him. My parents have never been the type to fuss about grades and homework. "It's fine," I say again.

Vicky clears her throat. "We had a phone call from your school."

"You did? Why?" I'm scanning my memory for incidents that might result in a phone call, but I'm coming up blank. I haven't done anything.

"From Mrs. Paulsen."

"Oh. I saw her once, right after Jeremy's...right after he fell. But that's all." *And I thought that kind of thing was supposed to be confidential.* "She just gave me some information about suicide and stuff."

Vicky looks uncomfortable. "I guess a couple of your teachers have spoken to her. Apparently they're concerned about you. Do you know what they might be noticing?"

Oh, nothing. Just me crying in class and spending half the day in the bathroom. Just me turning into zombie girl. I shrug. "It's been hard, you know? I'm okay though. I mean, I'm not...you know."

"Not what?"

"Not going to do what Jeremy did." I don't want to be having this conversation.

"You know you can always talk to us." Bill's eyebrows are almost touching, his frown lines deep furrows. "Always, Mel. About anything."

"I know," I say. "I just don't have anything to say."

There's a long, uncomfortable silence. Finally Vicky sighs. "Mrs. Paulsen said to remind you that you can talk to her anytime too. If you don't feel you can talk to us. Sometimes it's easier to talk to someone outside your family."

I shake my head. "No. I mean, that's nice of her, but there's nothing to talk about. Jeremy's just messed up. That's all."

"You're not blaming yourself for what happened, are you?" Vicky's voice is hesitant, like she's expecting me to flip out, like I'm such a mess that they have to walk on eggshells around me now.

"No. Is that what Mrs. Paulsen told you?"

She shakes her head. "No."

"Because it's really none of her business."

"Fine. Don't talk to her, then. But don't bottle things up."

I push my chair back from the table and stand up. "Can we please talk about something else?"

Vicky sighs. "Don't shut us out, Mel. Please."

"There's nothing to say," I tell her. It comes out louder than I mean it to. "Anyway, you wouldn't understand."

"Are you kidding me?" Vicky raises her voice, which she almost never does. Bill reaches over and puts a hand on her arm, but she shakes it off. "Believe me, Mel, I know what it is like to not be able to save someone. I know all about survivor guilt."

And that stuns me into silence.

~~~

Up in my room that night, I find myself reading the book Mrs. Paulsen lent me. Specifically, the section on survivor guilt. I hate that there is a name for it. I hate that it is so commonplace, so predictable. Apparently my anger at Jeremy is also *normal*. None of this really makes me feel less guilty. None of this changes the facts:

I suggested songs for his suicide playlist, suggested the bridge as a good way to go, even joined him for a last meal while stupidly thinking it was a date.

The author of the book, Dr. Miriam Issenman, says I have a right to be angry. Dr. Issenman doesn't have a clue, because she assumes that suicide or suicide attempts are not, in fact, the fault of the people left behind to read her book. Just like everyone is so sure I'm not to blame, so quick to reassure me that what Jeremy did wasn't my fault. But there were a million clues, and I just ignored them all. I refused to see that he was actually serious.

I pull out my phone and flip through the photos until I find a shot I snapped of Jeremy the day we went to the beach. He's looking right at me, eyebrows raised, the wind blowing his dark hair away from his face, his lips curved in a slight smile. Behind him, out of focus, is the gray-green water that his brother drowned in.

If Jeremy calls, I tell myself, I will keep it together. I'll be calm, supportive; I'll let him know that I will always be there for him. I won't ask about Kamala and I won't freak out about him letting Suzy down.

If there is anyone I should be angry with, it is myself.

Running Away

For a whole week, Jeremy doesn't come home. He doesn't call, doesn't text, doesn't even let me know he's alive. I call his mom and she tells me curtly that he's still away. He's probably with that girl, Kamala—but I can't stop wondering if he might have just wandered off, taken an overdose of something, be lying dead in the bushes somewhere.

And then, on Sunday evening, he shows up at my front door. With a shaved head.

I actually don't recognize him for a few seconds. Without his black hair flopping over his forehead, he looks completely different. His Adam's apple juts out sharply in his throat, and there are hollows at his temples and beneath his sharp cheekbones. He looks like someone who's dying of cancer or AIDS.

"Jeremy?" I say.

"Hi, Mel. What's up?"

Like we just saw each other yesterday. Like he hasn't been missing in action for a week. Like he hasn't scared the hell out of me and everyone else who cares about him.

"Actually, I've been kind of worried," I say.

"Don't be. Everything's good." He grins. "Better than good, actually."

I step back. "Are you coming in?"

Jeremy follows me into the kitchen and I pour us two glasses of water. "Bill and Vicky went out for dinner," I tell him. "They should be back soon. Are you hungry?"

"No, I'm fine. Thanks." He takes a glass from me and sits down at the kitchen table.

I sit across from him, feeling awkward. "So, where've you been?"

"Gainesville."

"With that girl?" I try to keep my voice neutral, like I'm just curious.

"Kamala. Yeah, and her friends. They're all Hare Krishnas." He leans toward me. "It's amazing, Mel. It's so beautiful."

"So what do they do? I mean, they chant, right?" I picture the videos I watched on YouTube—the rhythm of the voices, the ecstatic expressions. "And what's with the shaved head?"

He runs his hand over his scalp self-consciously. "Feels funny. It's just supposed to be cleaner, is all. And it shows, you know, that you're committed."

"Are you?" I guess if he's happy, I should be too—but instead I feel like I might start to cry.

Jeremy's eyes are shining. "It was the most incredible thing, Mel. The chanting. I mean, I was a bit skeptical, but I went along with it, you know? And after a few minutes— I mean, not long at all—it was like all that stuff—all that noise in my head—just went away. No anxiety, no fear, nothing. Just peaceful." He pauses, looking up at the ceiling as if he's reliving the moment in his mind. "I was so overwhelmed. I actually started crying."

"Hmm." It totally sounds like a cult. "So then what happened?"

"Oh, there was music and dancing. And someone spoke. He read some stuff from the Bhagavad Gita, and actually a few Bible verses too. He talked about ignorance, and how it keeps us trapped, and how we have to pay attention to our thoughts and make sure we are thinking right thoughts."

"*Right thoughts*? Sounds a bit Orwellian."

"No, no. It's not like that. It's just that, um, thinking wrong thoughts keeps us stuck in ignorance. Kamala says we need to free ourselves from illusions, and we can't do that if we are thinking that our bodies are our real selves or that the material world is all there is." He leans toward me, elbows on the table, chin resting on his knuckles. "She says that we get stuck pursuing material goals based on selfish desires, but when Krishna consciousness and love of God start to awaken in our hearts, we lose interest in these temporary things."

I take a sip of my water and move the glass around on the table, watching the sliding water circles it leaves behind. "So, are you and Kamala, like, an item?"

He sits back and shakes his head. "Actually, it's frowned upon."

"*Frowned upon?* What, sex?"

"Yeah. It ties us to the material world."

I snort. "So you took a vow of celibacy or something?"

"It's not like that, Mel." He sounds so earnest. "It's just that it doesn't help you develop true Krishna consciousness."

"Right." I think of him kissing me, right before he decided to drive to the Suicide Bridge. "You know, I've been kind of freaking out all week."

"You have? Why?"

"Seriously?" I stare at him. "Because you disappeared, Jeremy. Because you were supposed to be gone for one evening and that was last weekend. Because you didn't answer my calls or my texts."

"My phone battery was dead and I didn't have my charger."

"And you stood up Suzy. The kid I babysit, remember?"

He looks blank.

"You were supposed to come over on Monday and talk to her. About bullying and stuff?"

"Oh yeah. Shit." His hand goes to his forehead, to tug on the lock of hair that is no longer there. "I totally forgot."

"I noticed. So did she." I scowl at him, remembering my panicked call to his mother. "And you know what, Jeremy? When you disappear, people worry. Especially, you know, after what happened before."

"I told you, I won't do anything like that again."

"Fine. That doesn't mean I won't worry."

He sighs. "Can we just move on, Mel? I mean, I came over to tell you how great it all was. Can't you just be happy for me?"

A dark anger is boiling up in my chest, threatening to spill out. I clench my fists under the table, push them against my thighs. "I guess I don't think it's so great," I say stiffly.

"You have to come next time. Meet these people, try chanting with them. It's like nothing else, Mel. I can't explain how good it feels."

"It's cowardly," I say. "You're just running away from things like you always do. Like you did that day we went to look for your father. Remember that? You lost your nerve and ran away, and look how that day ended up. With you jumping off a bridge."

He leans toward me. "I need to talk to my father. I know that. But the bridge...I think that had to happen, Mel.

Because that's when I realized that I wanted to live. And I did, which is crazy, right? People jump off that bridge and die all the time. But not me."

I stand up so abruptly that my chair tips over backward, crashing to the tile floor. "You weren't saved for a reason, Jeremy. It was pure, freaky, dumb luck."

"I don't think so," he says.

"No. You think you were saved so that you could dance around chanting in fucking saffron robes," I spit out. "Which is fucking crazy, Jeremy."

He stands up too, more slowly, one hand pushed against his ribs. "Mel."

"I know you feel like shit about your brother, okay? I get that."

"That's got nothing to do with this."

"Bullshit," I say. "It has everything to do with it. You think I don't know how shitty it feels to accept that you should have saved someone and you didn't?"

"Mel," he says again. "Mel..."

I realize I am crying. "Sometimes you can't save people, Jeremy. Like Ramon."

"What are you talking about? What does Ramon have to do with this?"

"Everything," I say. "Remember when we first met and you wrote me that note? You signed it *your compatriot on death row*."

"It was a joke, Mel. You know that."

"But it's true, right? So maybe you should just accept that we're all going to end up dead and do something useful with the time you have."

He folds his arms across his chest, his face tight with anger. "And let me guess: you're going to decide what is useful and what isn't."

"Showing up to help Suzy would have been useful," I say. "Keeping your promise to an eight-year-old would be useful. Letting a kid like that down is a pretty big fail."

"There is no failure for one who pleases Krishna."

I want to slap his smug face. "Oh, did Kamala tell you that?"

Jeremy runs his hands over his scalp. "Is that what this is about? You're jealous?"

"No. I'm pissed off, Jeremy. I'm pissed off that you're being so selfish. I'm pissed off that you survived that fall but you're still throwing your life away." My voice is getting louder and louder, and every time I look at his shaved head, I want to hit him. "I mean, Hare Krishnas? Really? Because if all you care about is that it makes you feel good, you might as well just start shooting heroin."

There's a noise behind me, and I turn around. My parents are standing in the entrance to the kitchen, their jackets still on, eyes wide with concern. I wonder how much they've heard.

"Sorry to intrude," Bill says. "Good to see you again, Jeremy."

"You too." Jeremy clears his throat. "I should go."

"Fine," I say.

"Don't feel you need to rush off because of us," Vicky says.

"No, really, I…" Jeremy nods awkwardly and backs away from me, then turns and heads for the door. I watch him leave without a word.

Vicky puts her hand on my shoulder. "Are you all right?"

"Yes. No. Not really." My throat closes up, squeezing off the flow of words.

"I didn't recognize him at first," she says. "The hair."

I nod.

"I'll put the kettle on," Bill says. "Make some tea."

"Good idea." Vicky looks me in the eyes, her gaze steady. "Should we leave you alone? Or do you want to talk about it?"

I shrug. I don't know what I want.

"We didn't mean to eavesdrop," Bill says. "But I couldn't help catching a few words."

"It's okay," I say. "I guess we were shouting."

Bill pulls three mugs out of the cupboard and drops a tea bag in each. Then he turns to face me, leaning against the counter behind him. "Is he using drugs, honey?"

"Drugs? No."

"I don't mean to pry, but I thought I heard you say something about heroin."

I stare at him for a second, trying to remember. "Oh. No, he's not."

Vicky tilts her head, watching me. "Are you sure? You know you can tell us anything..."

"I was just saying he might as well be." There's a long silence and my words hang in the air. It sounds awful—me yelling stuff like that at someone who has just survived a suicide attempt. "He's throwing his life away anyway," I say defensively.

Bill gets the milk out of the fridge. "You taking sugar these days?"

"No." I pick up my tipped-over chair, sit down at the table and lean my chin on my hands. "I know I shouldn't have said that to him. You don't have to tell me."

Vicky sits across from me, in the seat Jeremy just left. "I wasn't going to say anything of the sort."

I swallow and feel the throat-ache of held-back tears. "He's joined the Hare Krishnas," I say. The kettle starts to whistle, but not before I hear a low chuckle from Bill. "It's not funny," I say. "It's a cult. He's totally brainwashed."

Bill pours water into the three mugs and carries them over to the table. "Sorry. I shouldn't have laughed. It's just that I went through a little phase like that at university."

"*You* did?" I can't picture my father chanting. Or shaving his head or giving up steak.

My mother looks surprised. "I don't think you've even told me about this."

He shrugs. "*Phase* might be overstating it. I went to a couple of meetings, tried to read the Bhagavad Gita."

"Why?" I ask him.

Bill looks apologetic. "I'd like to say it was part of a great philosophical search for life's deeper meaning, but the truth is, someone invited me to go and I wanted to make some friends."

"Um…"

"I was underage," he says. "I couldn't go to the bar."

Vicky laughs. "How long did that last?"

"Oh, all of a week or two." He looks at me. "Sounds like you think Jeremy might be in a bit deeper."

"He's probably pretty vulnerable," Vicky says. "Mel, do you really think it's a cult?"

"I don't know. Aren't all religions kind of cults?"

"You know what I mean. Are you concerned about him?"

"Of course I am." I'm suddenly feeling exhausted. "But I don't think anyone's twisting his arm or taking his money, if that's what you mean."

Bill pours milk into my tea and his own, puts the jug back in the fridge and sits down at the table with

Vicky and me. "We all have to make sense of things in our own way, love. I don't suppose this will do him any harm. Maybe it'll help him find some kind of peace with everything."

"How can it? I mean, isn't it a way of not facing things?"

"What do you mean?" Vicky asks. "What is it you think he should be doing?"

"I don't know." I blink back tears. "I just want him back the way he was before all this happened."

"Which means what? How was he different?" Vicky says.

I remember his obsession with lucid dreaming, his belief in reincarnation, his conviction that his brother was communicating with him through his dreams. "Maybe he wasn't. I don't know...He just doesn't deal with reality. He doesn't accept that his brother is dead."

"Mmm. Hard thing to accept."

"I think believing stuff like this is what got him into trouble in the first place," I say. "Like, he thought if he jumped off the bridge, he'd be with his brother again."

"Did he tell you that?"

There's a long silence. I can feel my heart thumping. "I should have known he was going to do it," I whisper. "I should've been able to stop him."

"Honey," Bill breaks in. "You can't blame yourself."

"You don't know!" My face and arms are ice cold and tingling, like all the blood in my body is rushing to fuel my racing heart. "You don't know what I knew. You don't know all the things I said to him."

"Regardless—" Bill starts to speak but stops as my mother puts her hand on his arm.

"Let her finish," she says.

And they both sit there, silent, waiting.

If I don't tell them now, I never will. If I don't let this out right now, I will keep it hidden forever, wrapping layer after layer of lies around it. I'll carry it with me always, like a glossy pearl with poison in its heart, and it'll slowly kill me. "It was my idea," I whisper, so quietly that both my parents lean in, straining to catch my words. "I said it first. One day at school. He was down about something and I said...I said, *We can jump off the Skyway Bridge together.*"

I can see the flinch, the tightening of the skin under Vicky's eyes. "Did you mean it?"

"No. But I said it."

"People joke about things," Bill says. "That's normal. People say, *I'd rather die than sit through another faculty meeting.* Or *I'll slit my wrists if I have to listen to one more student whine about a B+.* It doesn't mean you're suggesting that anyone actually kill themselves."

"We talked about what we'd have for our last meal," I say. My face is hot, my eyes stinging, but even this last humiliating detail is spilling out. "We went to a restaurant. And I thought it was, you know, a date."

"Oh, Mel," Vicky says. "Honey."

"I thought...I don't know what I thought." I start to cry. "I didn't know he meant it. I didn't know he'd actually...Even that night, on the bridge...I didn't think he'd jump."

My mother's arms are around me, holding me tightly.

"None of this makes it your fault," Bill says. "None of it."

"He made a choice," Vicky says.

"I should've known." My voice is muffled against her shoulder.

"Maybe," Vicky says, and I am so surprised I pull away and look at her face. She touches my cheek. "If you were older, maybe. If you had more experience dealing with people going through all kinds of problems. But Mel, I'm a counselor. I have a master's degree; I spent years working with people who are dealing with depression and all kinds of trauma; I took a whole course in suicide prevention. And you know what? I've still lost clients to suicide. More than once."

"I bet you didn't suggest to anyone that they jump off the bridge," I say.

"No," she says. She gives me a tentative grin, just a twitch of one corner of her mouth. "But that's because I'm a trained professional."

"God, Vicky." I don't know whether I'm laughing or crying or both. "This isn't funny."

"I know. I know." She holds my gaze. "It's awful. And that's why, sometimes, you have to laugh. You should hear the jokes on death row."

"They joke about dying?"

"They have to."

I nod. "I always thought Jeremy was joking. Because school is so awful sometimes, and because of everything that happened with his brother and his dad. I was just joking about dying, you know? I thought he was too."

"Maybe he was," Bill says, his voice a low rumble. "Maybe he wasn't serious either until that moment on the bridge. Maybe it was impulsive. Not planned."

"You think?" I'd feel better, somehow, if I believed that. Less stupid and less responsible.

Bill shrugs. "Why don't you ask him?"

I think about the fight we just had, the words I can't take back—*cowardly, crazy, selfish*—and I wonder if I'll get the chance.

Letting Go

After our fight, I don't call Jeremy and he doesn't call me. A few days go by, and then a week. I meet up with Adriana one evening and we drink my dad's milkshakes and go for a walk together. Bill and Vicky seem so happy to see her, but it's all a bit awkward and stilted and oddly boring, and I don't know how much we really have in common now. Being with her makes me feel lonely. It makes me miss Jeremy. Still, it is good not to be enemies anymore. Before she gets on the bus to go home, I tell her that I understand why she called the ambulance that night, and that even though I'd rather she hadn't, I think she did the right thing. She just nods and says thanks, but the relief on her face when she says it makes me want to cry.

I get through my days at school, still feeling like zombie girl. I visit Mrs. Paulsen's office once and sit in the pale blue chair and stare at the kitten poster and wonder how much longer I'll have to hang on before I start feeling normal again. I tell her about Jeremy and the Hare Krishnas. I don't cry. She says that Jeremy will have to find his own way through and that I need to focus on myself. She says if I still feel like this in a few weeks, maybe I should think about seeing my doctor. I ask if that's code for taking antidepressants, and she laughs and says it might be. She's nice, but it feels weird to talk to a stranger, and I don't think I'll go back. Unless I feel worse, I guess.

Every day after school, I hang out with Suzy. It's the best part of my day, actually. Suzy's the one person who doesn't know about Jeremy, and it's a huge relief just to be with her and listen to her talk about stars and galaxies and her new passion, the 1920s. We spend hours poring over websites together, learning about the postwar economic boom, flappers, jazz, fashion, Art Deco. We print out images of young women in New York, New Orleans, Paris and Berlin. Suzy prints out photographs of the actress Louise Brooks, gets her dark hair cut in a short bob, draws young women in sleeveless dresses with low waistlines and decides she might be a fashion designer instead of an astronomer. "*I'm* never going to smoke though," she tells me, drawing a cloud of smoke above the waifish girl she is sketching.

"Good," I say. "I should hope not."

"I like the cigarette holders though," she says wistfully.

I roll my eyes.

"You think it would be a weird thing to collect?" She adds a fancy carved cigarette holder to her drawing.

"Cigarette holders?" I laugh. "No weirder than stamps or baseball cards. Less weird than Beanie Babies. Anyway, who cares if it's weird? I like weird."

"I don't know if my mom would let me."

"Ask her."

She nods. "They didn't know back then."

"Didn't know what?"

"That smoking killed you." She points at the black-and-white image on the screen of her laptop: an old photograph of a crowded New Orleans jazz club, young men and women laughing, wreathed with smoke. "Look at them. They thought it was glamorous." She looks up at me, her big eyes ringed with her mom's eyeliner. "Have you ever smoked, Mel?"

"No," I tell her, lying without hesitation. "No way."

"Good," she says. "Because I want you to live for a long, long, long time."

"Me too," I say, and I realize that despite everything, and unlike my previous statement, this is true.

The doorbell rings. Suzy wrinkles her nose. "I know who that is," she says.

"Who?"

"Jehovah's Witnesses."

I laugh. "Why do you say that?"

"Because they came a couple of weeks ago and I invited them in," she says. "Mom was mad, but I wanted to hear what they had to say."

"And?"

She shrugs. "Boring, boring, boring. And now they keep coming back and Mom's too polite to tell them to get lost."

"I'm not though." I hate people pushing their beliefs on other people, so I'd be more than happy to let them know they're not welcome. I head toward the door, Suzy behind me giggling nervously. "Don't worry," I tell her. "I won't be rude. I'll just tell them not to come back."

I open the door—

—and there is Jeremy.

"Hey, it's you!" Suzy says. "What happened to your hair?"

"I cut it off," he says. "And so did you, I see. Yours looks better than mine."

She touches her bobbed hair. "I'm a flapper now."

"I like it. And I'm very sorry I'm late," he tells her.

"Really late," she says. "Like, more than a week late, I think! But that's okay. Do you still like ice cream?"

"It's one of my favorite things," he says solemnly. He turns to me. "Vicky told me you were here. Sorry I didn't call first."

"No problem," I say. "Did you want to come in?"

"Sure."

Jeremy sits down at the kitchen table. I help Suzy dish out three bowls of rainbow sherbet, and I sneak glances at Jeremy, trying to figure out if he's angry with me, wondering if the fact that his scalp is now covered with a short dark fuzz means anything at all. If he starts telling Suzy about Krishna consciousness, I'll kill him.

Suzy takes two bowls to the table, slides one over to Jeremy and sits down beside him. "Mel's babysitting me every day, did she tell you? I don't go to after-school care anymore."

Jeremy nods. "Is that good?"

"Very good. It'd be better if I didn't have to go to school at all though."

"I don't go anymore," he says.

I shake my head at him. How is that helpful? It's not like Suzy has a choice.

"Are you going to go back?" she asks him.

"Nope."

"Never?"

He shakes his head. "I don't think so."

"What about university?"

Jeremy scoops a spoonful of neon-orange ice cream into his mouth. "What about it?"

Suzy looks at him pityingly. "You can't go to university if you don't finish high school."

"I'm not planning to go to university. Not everyone has to, you know."

"I want to," Suzy says firmly. "I'd go right now if I could. Did you know that MIT is one of the best places in the whole world to study astronomy?"

"That's what you want to do?"

"Maybe. Or fashion design."

"Hmm." He licks the back of his spoon thoughtfully. "Melody told me you didn't like school."

"I don't like *elementary* school," she says.

"No, neither did I." He looks at me, like he's wondering how much he should say. "Kids can be pretty mean. That's how it was for me anyway."

"Did Mel tell you what the kids call me?" Suzy looks at him, and then at me. I shake my head and she turns back to him. "Poo! They call me Poo."

He frowns. "Like Winnie the Pooh?"

"No. Like the other kind. You know." Suzy stabs at her melting ice cream with her spoon, once, twice, three times. "I hate them."

"Maybe they have their own stuff going on," he says.

"What do you mean?"

I watch his face—the blue-purple smudges under his dark eyes, the tracery of veins at his temples, the sharp edge of his Adam's apple as he swallows—and wonder what he is thinking.

"Just problems in their own lives," he says. "At home, maybe."

"Like maybe their parents are getting divorced? Or they hit their kids, even?"

"Maybe." He shrugs. "Seems like people who are happy mostly treat other people well."

Suzy ponders this, slowly stirring her ice cream into a sludgy soup. After a long minute she looks up at him. "There are a lot of kids who are mean to me. A lot."

"Maybe there are a lot of people who are unhappy," he says.

I'm not sure how this is a helpful thought—it's hardly cheerful anyway—but Suzy looks interested. "In my school? Or in the world?"

"Maybe both."

"You think they can't help being mean?"

"I think sometimes when people are very unhappy, they don't really think about other people at all. They feel so bad that they forget that other people have feelings too. And they hurt them without really meaning to." Jeremy turns and looks at me as he answers. "Sometimes they're so unhappy that they do awful things. Things that hurt other people."

Is he talking about himself? And me?

Suzy isn't buying it. "They don't call me Poo by accident," she says.

He turns back to her. "No. But maybe they aren't really thinking about how it makes you feel."

"I've told them I don't like it," she says.

"That's good," I say. "It's good that you stand up for yourself."

"But it doesn't make them stop."

Jeremy nods. "When I was your age, the kids called me Spaz. And Retard."

"That's awful." Suzy dips her spoon in her ice-cream soup and licks it clean again. "Not as bad as Poo though."

"It gets better," he tells her.

"When?"

"Um, high school? I guess that seems like a long way off."

"It *is* a long way off."

"Maybe you'll make a friend soon," I say. "Even if some kids are still mean, it'll be better if you have someone you can count on."

"Like you and Jeremy," she says.

Jeremy looks at me and our eyes meet. His are shining with tears.

"Yeah," I say, and my voice cracks a little. "Like me and Jeremy."

He stands. "I should go."

"I'll walk you out," I say.

Jeremy gives Suzy a quick hug goodbye, which to my surprise she doesn't seem to mind, and I follow him to the front door. "Jeremy? Are you okay?"

He nods. "Yeah. I meant what I said. I'm really sorry, Mel."

I follow him out the door and onto the porch, so that Suzy won't hear us.

"For what?"

"All of it. Being so wrapped up in myself, I guess. Not really seeing you. Putting you through that, you know? Seeing me jump." He shakes his head. "Selfish, right?"

"I'm sorry too," I say. I can feel my throat getting tight, feel tears threatening. "I should've stopped you. I didn't think you'd do it." I remember my dad saying *ask him,* but I'm scared of what he might say.

He answers the question anyway. "I don't think I knew I was going to do it until we got there. Until we were actually standing on the bridge, looking down."

I'm right back there, seeing the blackness below, feeling his hand slip free of mine. "Why did you do it?" I whisper.

He looks me right in the eyes. "Honestly? I don't know."

"You jumped off a bridge." My voice cracks and trembles on the edge of a sob. "How can you not know why?"

"I've been seeing this counselor. And I keep coming up with explanations, you know? But I feel like I'm just making up stories for him to write in his notes. About Lucas, about my mother, about my dad." He hesitates. "He never even came to see me. At the hospital, you know? Mom talked to him, but he didn't come."

"Asshole," I say. "That's awful."

"I mean, I've talked to the counselor about all this. I get that there's reasons that I could be depressed or whatever." His eyes search mine, like he's trying to figure out if I understand. "But trying to link it to that night? That's where it feels like I'm making stuff up. Because none of it really explains why I did it."

"So what does explain it? What does your counselor say?" I know I'm pushing him for an answer he maybe doesn't have, but I can't stop. I need to know the reason why. "I mean, what was going through your mind that night?"

"When we were on that bridge, looking down? Nothing." He shrugs. "Letting go seemed easier than holding on."

$$\approx$$

When I get home, Vicky and Bill are sitting together watching a movie in the living room, a bowl of popcorn balanced on the arm of the couch. Bill hits the Pause button on the remote when he sees me come in. "Hey."

"Popcorn for dinner?" I say.

"Nothing better. Join us? We just started the movie; it's supposed to be good."

I nod, and they slide apart to make room for me between them. I sit down, feeling both their concern and their effort to not show it.

"Everything okay?" Bill asks.

"Yeah." I look at him and then at Vicky. "Actually, yeah. Like, not perfect, but okay enough."

They both wait, Bill's thumb hovering over the Play button.

"Jeremy came over to Suzy's," I say.

"You guys are talking again?" Vicky asks.

"We weren't ever *not* talking, exactly," I say. "But yeah." She squeezes my knee.

"Play the movie," I say, and I let myself relax into the space between them.

≋

That night, in my room, I pull out the book Jeremy loaned me earlier this fall: *The Myth of Sisyphus and Other Essays*. I never did read it, but now I lie on my couch, open the book and immediately recognize the first words:

There is but one truly serious philosophical problem and that is suicide. Judging whether life is or is not worth living amounts to answering the fundamental question of philosophy.

Jeremy quoted this to me the very first time we met, and I said, mockingly, that Shakespeare said it first. I find myself flipping through the pages, not reading methodically but getting pulled in here and there, clinging to the words as if they might somehow explain Jeremy to me. I know it's stupid; I know the answers aren't going to be in here.

Here's *The Myth of Sisyphus*, Cliff's Notes version: The gods cursed Sisyphus to push this huge boulder up a mountain, and then, when he'd finally get it to the top, it'd roll back down and he'd have to start all over again. Such is life, I guess—not the most cheerful worldview. And then my eyes fall on a sentence harshly underlined in black ink, the pen pressed so hard it's dented the pages: *Forever I shall be a stranger to myself.*

And maybe that's all the answer I'm going to get. Maybe Jeremy can't tell me why because he doesn't know. He never knew. All our conversations about suicide— about Camus, the bridge, the playlist and the last meal— I'd thought maybe they had put the idea in his head. But if the idea wasn't already there, we wouldn't have had those conversations in the first place. Maybe in the end, the plan didn't matter as much as the impulse. That moment on the bridge, when he jumped and I didn't.

I chose to live. He chose to let go.

Maybe *why* didn't matter. Maybe it wasn't even the right question.

I pick up my phone and call Jeremy. It's kind of late, but he picks up on the first ring. "Mel?"

"Jeremy? You're not going to do it again, are you?"

"I don't think so."

Forever I shall be a stranger to myself. "Really really don't think so?"

He actually laughs. "Really *really* really."

"Good."

"Is that why you called?"

"Sort of. I was reading that book you loaned me. Camus."

"Oh yeah. Poor old Sisyphus."

"It's depressing."

"Did you read it all?"

"Just skimmed," I say. "It's kind of dense."

"You should read the last bit," Jeremy tells me.

"Does it get less depressing?"

"In a way. He says you have to imagine Sisyphus happy. Accepting it all."

"Yeah?" I flip through the pages. "I'll try to read it," I say, although I already know I probably won't. I prefer novels, and I have stacks of good ones—birthday presents, last year's Christmas presents—that I haven't got around to reading yet. "Listen, do you want to get together? Maybe tomorrow night? Or..."

There's a pause. Too long a pause. "Um, I'd like to see you, but I can't tomorrow."

I wait.

"I'm going up to Gainesville for a few days."

"The Hare Krishnas?"

"Yeah."

"Okay," I say. "Give me a call when you get back. You know, if you want."

"Sure." I can hear the relief in his voice. I guess he was afraid I'd freak out again. "I'll call you. I'll probably stay up there over the weekend, but maybe Monday or Tuesday we could do something. Go to the beach. Take Suzy, maybe, if you want."

"She'd like that."

"Yeah?"

"Thanks for visiting her," I say.

"Yeah, well, about time, right?"

"Right."

He laughs. "I'll talk to you soon, then?"

"Yeah," I say. "I'll be here."

Acknowledgments

Thanks to my fabulous editor, Sarah Harvey, for her always astute guidance; to my coffee-shop writing buddies, Kari Jones and Alex Van Tol, for their inspiration and insights; and to my wonderful family for endless love and support.

ROBIN STEVENSON is the author of seventeen novels for teens and children. Her young adult novels include *Hummingbird Heart, Escape Velocity, Inferno, Out of Order* and Governor General's Award finalist *A Thousand Shades of Blue*. Robin was born in England, grew up mostly in Ontario and now lives on the west coast of Canada, with her partner and son. She enjoys visiting schools and offers creative-writing classes for people of all ages. Robin loves hearing from readers and can be reached through her website at www.robinstevenson.com.

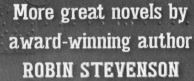
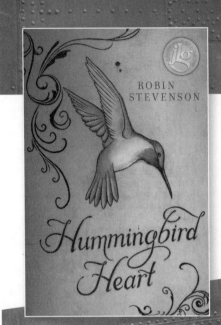

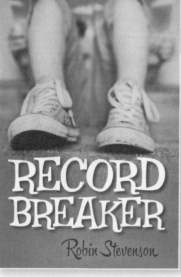

2009 Governor General's Literary Award Nominee

"The writing's emotional honesty and realistic dialogue will appeal to many teens."
—*Booklist*

9781551439211 pb
9781551439235 pdf
9781554695669 epub

2014 Silver Birch Award Winner

"A quiet novel that delves into difficult subjects, Stevenson's latest shines a warm light on both grief and friendship...A thoughtful evocation of an uneasy time on both a personal and global level."
—*Booklist*

9781554699599 pb • 9781554699605 pdf
9781554699612 epub

ORCA BOOK PUBLISHERS
www.orcabook.com • 1-800-210-5277